SWEET REUNION

STACY CLAFLIN

SWEET REUNION
INDIGO BAY SWEET ROMANCE SERIES #11
by Stacy Claflin
http://www.stacyclaflin.com

Copyright ©2018 Stacy Claflin. All rights reserved.
Cover by Najla Qamber Designs
www.najlaqamberdesigns.com
Edited by Staci Troilo

This is a work of fiction. Any resemblance to actual persons living or dead, businesses, events, or locales is purely coincidental or used fictitiously. The author has taken great liberties with locales including the creation of fictional towns.

INDIGO BAY SWEET ROMANCE
SERIES

What is the Indigo Bay Sweet Romance Series? It's tons of fun for readers! But more specifically, it is a series of books written by authors who love romance. Grab a glass of sweet tea, sit on the porch, and get ready to be swept away into this charming South Carolina beach town.

The Indigo Bay world has been written so readers can dive in anywhere in the series without missing a beat. Read one or all—they're all sweet, fun rides that you won't soon forget. Also, as special treats, you'll see some recurring characters. How many can *you* find?

Sweet Dreams by Stacy Claflin
Sweet Matchmaker by Jean Oram
Sweet Sunrise by Kay Correll
Sweet Illusions by Jeanette Lewis
Sweet Regrets by Jennifer Peel
Sweet Rendezvous by Danielle Stewart

CHAPTER 1

Magnolia Kendrick jumped from the booth and darted between the tables, avoiding waiters and waitresses. She didn't slow until she reached the bathroom. Closing the stall door behind her, she leaned against the wall and took in a deep breath of heavily-sweetened air.

That had been close. Too close.

Once her heart rate returned to normal, she exited the stall. An older lady shot her a glare. Probably because she hadn't heard a flush.

Maggie flashed her a quick smile and went to the mirror to fix her makeup, though it didn't need it. She only needed another minute or two to pull herself together before rejoining Aunt Lucille—the reason she'd fled to the bathroom.

Auntie had a good heart, bless her, but the woman couldn't take a clue. Or a flat-out request.

Maggie would just have to try again. What other option was there? She lived with her great-aunt, who had tried to set her up with practically every eligible bachelor in Indigo Bay.

Now at Figaro's, the restaurant owned by a distant cousin

about half an hour from their town, Auntie was attempting another set-up.

Lord have mercy. It was almost enough for Maggie to head back home to Georgia—to the one place she could never show her face again.

Almost.

Maggie wanted nothing to do with a relationship of any kind. That was part of the reason she'd moved to Indigo Bay. A fresh start in a town where people didn't know her problems.

She stood tall and practiced her smile. It was her best feature, unless she listened to the people who adored her too-thick and too-curly dark hair. Long as it was, it was a nightmare. But she hated the way she looked when it was shorter.

The bathroom door flung open. "Maggie!"

Maggie turned to find her cousin Savannah. It wasn't unusual to find a relative at Figaro's. "Hi, Savannah."

"Auntie said you might be in here."

Maggie put her makeup back in her purse. "Did she send you to find me?"

"She said you ran off like a chicken with its head cut off." Savannah raised an eyebrow, clearly wanting to know more.

"Can't a girl use the bathroom?" Maggie adjusted her skirt.

"Is everything okay, darlin'?"

It would be if Aunt Lucille would quit trying to set her up with every available bachelor within a twenty-mile radius of Indigo Bay.

Savannah stepped closer and put a hand on Maggie's arm. "Everyone worries about you, you know."

Maggie smiled as sugary sweet as she could. "I appreciate the concern, but I'm fine. Hey, Auntie wasn't talking to anyone, was she?"

Savannah fanned herself. "You mean that new server, Emilio?"

Wonderful. Aunt Lucille was probably planning Maggie's date with Emilio at that moment.

"You don't like him?" Savannah frowned.

Maggie sighed. "I don't even know him."

"I wouldn't mind getting to know him. Did you see those eyes? Blue as a clear lake."

"Must've missed those. Take care, okay? Say hello to Auntie Charlotte for me."

"I will." Savannah gave a little wave. "Tell me if you go out with Emilio. I want to hear all about it."

Maggie forced a smile. There would be no date. She'd managed to avoid all of Aunt Lucille's attempts. She could do it again. Maybe the tickle in her throat would turn into something more if she was lucky.

As her cousin headed for a stall, Maggie made her way out into the hallway. She'd far prefer to stay in the bathroom until lunch was over, but Auntie would just send more ladies after her until Maggie returned.

Maggie was so busy thinking about what she would say that she bumped into someone.

She looked up. "I'm so sorry. I didn't—"

Her gaze locked with a familiar but nearly-forgotten set of dark brown eyes that appeared as surprised to see her as she was to see them. Maggie's heart skipped a beat, then her pulse drummed through her body. Her cheeks warmed, heat spreading across her face.

Canyon Leblanc.

He still had the same effect on her he'd had so many years earlier, despite the fact that she'd nearly forgotten about him. Not because she'd wanted to, but because life had taken them their separate ways and they'd lost touch.

He was just as gorgeous as ever, if not more so. Tan,

neatly dressed. His dark hair was longer than it had been so many years before—and it suited him.

A waitress rushed by, bumping Maggie and nearly throwing her against her old friend. He still wore the same aftershave.

A wave of first-love emotions shoved their way to the surface. Feelings that had overwhelmed her younger self but she'd never allowed herself to act upon. Instead, she'd pined for him.

Then he'd exited from her life.

Now things had changed so much. Too much.

No doubt about it—he was definitely more attractive now. He'd grown out of his boyish good looks and had matured into a ruggedly handsome man. His deep brown eyes sent a shiver to her very core.

Maggie took a step back so she couldn't smell him. So she could think straight.

She didn't have the time to get distracted by a handsome face—especially not the one in front of her.

They'd been staring at each other for too long. Someone needed to say something.

Maggie cleared her throat. "Canyon?"

He stared at her, his expression practically unreadable. "Maggie."

She struggled to find words, so she cleared her throat again just to give herself another moment to think of something to say. "I didn't realize you were back in town. Just a pit stop?"

He shook his head. "Nope. I'm back for good. Here for a job interview, in fact."

"You are? I'll put in a good word. My cousin owns the restaurant."

"Really?" Canyon arched a brow.

Something about that simple act took her breath away.

4

She needed to get away, and quick. Preferably before Auntie saw him and tried to set up a date.

Maggie forced a smile. "I'd love to catch up sometime. I'm staying at Aunt Lucille's. Pop in and say hi when you get a chance. We can have some tea or walk the beach like we used to."

Why had she just said that? The last thing she needed was him surprising her for a visit, especially at home. Auntie would want to set them up.

Awkward.

He ran his fingers through his hair. "Okay. It'd be real nice to catch up. I'd better get going. Interview in a few minutes."

Maggie nodded. "Right. Good luck."

Canyon headed down the hallway toward the offices.

She watched until he was out of sight then headed back to the booth where Aunt Lucille was nearly done with her meal. At least she was alone. Maggie had grown tired of thinking up excuses to avoid dates with the men her aunt constantly tried to set her up with.

"What took you so long, Maggie?" Aunt Lucille tugged on her perfectly-styled blonde hair and waited for a reply.

Maggie slid back to her spot. "I kept running into people. You didn't have to send Savannah after me."

Aunt Lucille dabbed her mouth with a napkin. "You'd been in there so long."

She hadn't, but rather than argue, Maggie took a big bite of her salmon.

"Emilio is free this Saturday afternoon."

Maggie nearly choked on her fish. "Auntie, I appreciate your concern but—"

"But nothing. You aren't getting any younger and you need to get your mind off the past. Isn't that why you came to stay with me?"

5

"I'm twenty-four. There's plenty of time to figure out what to do with my life."

Aunt Lucille tilted her head and sighed. "Young people these days. You can marry rich and not have to worry about a career. In my day, ladies went to college to get their MRS degree."

Maggie shoved a piece of broccoli into her mouth before she said something that would start an argument.

Auntie got a dreamy look on her face, then started talking about her late husband and their courting days. It may as well have been a hundred years ago, as far removed as it was from Maggie's situation.

She fought back tears that threatened. Why couldn't her aunt realize how painful all this was? Dating wasn't going to solve Maggie's problems. Getting engaged again certainly wouldn't.

Maggie was done with men, period. She couldn't take any more heartbreak. Once she figured out what she wanted to do with her life, she could focus on that. But that was the problem.

Nothing made her happy. She couldn't escape the pain of her past no matter how hard she tried.

CHAPTER 2

C anyon Leblanc tapped his feet, unable to sit still since running into Maggie. He raked his fingers through his hair.

She'd taken his breath away. The girl had always had that effect on him, ever since they were kids.

Every year, Canyon had waited for the summers when she would come to Indigo Bay and stay with Lucille Sanderson, the older woman who was always up in everyone's business. Canyon had always avoided the aunt but had gone out of his way to spend time with Maggie.

As a kid, he'd been tall, skinny, and awkward. With a mouth full of braces and two left feet, he'd never had the nerve to ask Maggie out on a date. He'd wanted to. Oh, how he'd wanted to. But the thought of holding her hand had nearly sent him into cardiac arrest.

How things had changed. Everything had changed, except Maggie's beauty. He always knew she'd grow up to be exquisite—and she'd far exceeded his wildest imagination. He could get lost in those bright blue eyes, and her long hair looked so soft. Canyon had always wanted to run his fingers

7

through it. And that smile... it had forever been his weakness. Maggie could curl her lips up, ask anything, and he would turn to mush.

But they were still worlds apart, and now more so than ever. Not only did she come from money, but her sweet and innocent smile told him that she was far too good for him. Especially after his wild living the last seven years.

Canyon raked his fingers through his hair again. It was a nervous habit that had always annoyed his mom. He'd grown worse with it while being away from her reminders to stop.

He and Maggie were polar opposites, and once she caught wind of his lifestyle, she'd run in the opposite direction.

A woman in a black pencil skirt and a tight bun appeared in front of him. "Canyon Leblanc?"

He nodded. "Yes, ma'am."

"Mr. Sanderson will be ready to see you in about ten minutes."

"Thank you."

The woman gave a quick nod, then disappeared around a corner.

Maggie's words ran through his mind. *I'll put in a good word for you.*

Canyon groaned. He didn't want a job because someone had pity on him. Because his childhood friend had connections. But even more than that, he didn't want to work for her family.

No, he wanted to land a job because he had earned it.

Canyon rose and hurried out of Figaro's. He *could* do the job—any position they gave him—and do it well, but he couldn't have Maggie thinking he was hired because she'd talked with her cousin.

He climbed into his rusty Ford Taurus and headed back to Indigo Bay. Maybe he could find a job in the small beach town. There had to be something he could do. It would save on gas, at least. Figaro's was about a thirty-minute drive.

Once back in town, he passed his mom's little dilapidated home and went to the beach. He stayed in the car and watched the beachgoers. A few kids flew kites in a patch of grass. Couples strolled the shore, hand-in-hand. There was an intense game of volleyball off to the side.

Canyon's phone buzzed with a text. It was from his friend Archer.

Archer: Itching to come back?
Canyon: Nope, sorry.
Archer: Not the same w/o you!
Canyon: I'm done. Going to find work at home.
Archer: Boring.
Canyon: Haha.
Archer: Meet any hot chicks?
Canyon: I'm looking for a JOB.
Archer: Doesn't mean you can't have both.
Canyon: Don't you have work to do?
Archer: On break. So many babes this week.
Canyon: Can't talk me back.
Archer: Bored w/o you here.
Canyon: Think up trouble yourself.
Archer: Give me some ideas.
Canyon: How about sleep? They work you to the bone.
Archer: Don't I know it. Cutting out now.
Canyon: Have fun.
Archer: You'll be back in a week. You can't stay away.
Canyon: This time I am.
Archer: Gonna eat those words.
Canyon: Wanna bet?
Archer: There's the Canyon we all love. You show up here, you owe me $50.
Canyon: Deal.

Archer: Easiest money I ever made.

Canyon: Dream on. You're gonna owe ME $50.

Archer: You wish. Bikini headed my way. Later.

Canyon: Bye.

He tossed his phone on the passenger seat and sighed. Since seeing Maggie, chasing after women with the guys just didn't hold the appeal it used to.

Canyon had left the cruise line for many reasons. Wanting to settle down was one of them. Maybe not marry, but at least find a nice girl he could date long-term while holding down a job where he could have weekends off.

Traveling the world had been a blast, but working seven days a week serving spoiled vacationers had lost its appeal. Getting chewed out by a fourteen-year-old brat because she didn't have enough blankets a few weeks prior had been the last straw.

He'd given his notice, and now he was a free man. If "free" meant living with his mom at twenty-five while all his old buddies were either married with kids or out of state.

Canyon tapped the steering wheel. Where would he find a job in Indigo Bay?

CHAPTER 3

Maggie spread out the beach towel, lounged on top of it, and closed her eyes. The warmth of the sun's rays relaxed her. She needed it after Aunt Lucille had just about set up a date for her and Emilio for Saturday afternoon.

Maggie had made up an excuse about having a hair appointment at that time. Now she had to schedule an appointment she didn't need. Maybe she could get some highlights or a trim.

But that was only a Band-Aid for a much bigger problem. Auntie would just keep trying to set Maggie up, thinking that would solve all her problems. There was no convincing her that she was just making it worse for Maggie. The woman was certain marriage would fix everything.

It wouldn't. Maggie's failed engagement was proof of that. In fact, it was those painful memories that kept her fighting to stay single. That was what would bring the least amount of pain. She had nothing to offer a husband anyway. Once a man found out her secret, they would run screaming like Dan had.

If only she could find a job she liked. She'd gotten a business degree because she was going to help run Dan's business.

Stupid, stupid, stupid. Getting a degree for a man.

Maggie didn't want to be in business. She'd only wanted to spend more time with Dan. It would've been perfect, if she wasn't flawed.

Now she needed to figure out what she loved. All she'd done so far was find more things she didn't want to do. She'd worked as a lifeguard at the beach, taught at the preschool, volunteered at the Manor, and worked at Happy Paws pet shop.

That didn't leave many options. Indigo Bay was always busy in the spring and summer, and seasonal jobs tended to fill early. It was no longer early, and there wasn't a single 'now hiring' sign in any business. She'd looked.

Maggie shoved all thoughts from her mind and focused on the waves crashing against the shore. Kids giggled and shrieked in the distance at the musical sounds of an ice cream truck. Thumps and grunts sounded from a nearby volleyball match. The sun's rays grew warmer, almost massaging her.

It was like a slice of Heaven. A small escape from everything.

Laughter sounded, and conversation grew closer.

"Maggie?"

So much for her escape from reality. Maggie sat up and opened her eyes. As they adjusted, she recognized three of her friends.

"Mind if we sit with you?" Courtney asked. Her bulging belly made it hard to say no.

"Of course not." Maggie flashed her friends a welcoming grin.

The three women all dropped their bags and spread out towels. Courtney dug an umbrella into the sand and sat halfway in its shade. Isabella made a show of doing everything with her left hand to show off the boulder that was her new engagement ring. Laura did everything one-handed as she kept the other hand on the baby strapped to her. She too stuck a large umbrella into the ground.

Maggie made small talk with them as they settled in. She was grateful for the distraction of small-town gossip, even if it would only take her mind off everything momentarily.

Isabella rolled onto her back and held up her left hand, staring at the ring. "Did you guys hear that Canyon Leblanc is in town?"

"Really?" Courtney gasped. "He's actually visiting his poor mom?"

"I heard he's here to stay," Laura said.

Everyone looked at Maggie.

"Do you know?" Isabella asked.

"He's looking for work."

"I knew you'd know." Isabella smiled. "Temporary or full-time?"

"I'm not sure."

Courtney rolled onto her side and rested her hand on her belly. "I heard he turned into a womanizer while he was away. Wasn't he working on a cruise boat?"

Maggie shrugged and shifted her weight uncomfortably. "I wouldn't know. I lost track of him. Haven't spoken since high school."

"But you know he's looking for work." Laura arched a brow and unwrapped the now-fussing baby from her sling.

"I ran into him at Figaro's for a moment. That's all. Aside from that, we haven't seen each other in years."

"Did Miss Lucille try setting you up with him?" Courtney asked.

The three giggled.

Maggie didn't. She shook her head.

Isabella closed her eyes. "It's only a matter of time."

Laura held Maggie's gaze. "Do you think you'd want to go out with him? You two were so close."

Maggie drew patterns in the sand. "That was high school. Besides, I'm not looking for a relationship." Ever.

Laura tilted her head. "You're only making your auntie more determined to find you a guy. Mama said Miss Lucille was asking her about both my brothers."

Maggie groaned. "I don't know why she thinks I need a man so badly. I can only imagine what everyone thinks of me."

Courtney squeezed Maggie's knee. "Everyone loves you. You're the sweetest thing and totally adorable."

"Thanks." Maggie lay down and closed her eyes. Images of Dan breaking up with her played through her mind.

Being sweet and adorable wasn't enough. What she needed was to figure out what to do with her life, and soon. If she could show her aunt that she was happy with a career, maybe she'd let up and find a new hobby other than trying to set up Maggie with a guy.

But what did she want to do? That was the one question she just didn't have an answer to.

CHAPTER 4

M aggie set her fork down and turned to Aunt Lucille. "I'm going to turn in early tonight."

Auntie frowned. "There's a concert at the beach tonight. Why don't you go there? You'll have fun, and maybe you'll meet a nice young man."

Knots formed in Maggie's stomach. She pressed her palms against the table. "I'm not looking for a relationship. I don't want to find a man, nice or otherwise."

Aunt Lucille's brows knit together. "You aren't getting any younger."

"I don't care!" Maggie flung her napkin on the table. "I'm not looking for a man. I don't want another relationship. All I want is some space to figure out what to do with my life. That's why I came here to Indigo Bay. Not to get stuck with another guy."

"Well, I—"

"Excuse me." Tears blurred Maggie's vision as she pushed her chair back. "I just need to be left alone."

Maggie fled upstairs, barely able to keep the tears at bay until she reached her bedroom. She buried her face in her pillow to muffle the sobs. Her whole body shook as the unwanted tears refused to stop.

It wasn't that she hadn't moved on from the breakup of her engagement. She had. It'd been a couple years. With all honesty, she could say she didn't want Dan back. She would never take him back, even if he begged. Not that he would. Rumor had it that he was already engaged again.

What really hurt, if she was being honest with herself, was the fact that she would never again have a relationship. Dropping her dream of having a family of her own had been the hardest thing she'd ever done.

Like any other girl, she'd planned out her wedding— everything from the dress to flowers and songs and decor. She'd filled a Pinterest board full of things she liked, but it was all for naught.

Magnolia Kendrick would never get married. Never have the three kids she'd already named.

None of that was for her, no matter how much she wanted it. Correction, no matter how much she *had* wanted it.

What she needed was a job that would consume her. Take up all her attention from morning until night. It could be anything since she already knew business. That was her degree, after all.

She even knew the ins and outs of starting a new business since she'd done so much to get Dan's restaurant up and running. More than he had, in fact.

Maggie rolled over and wiped her face, smearing mascara along her hand. She took a deep breath, then plodded over to the window and stared at the water past the beach. Off in the distance, she could see the crowd gathering for the concert.

Maybe Aunt Lucille was right. It might do Maggie some good to head over there. Not to find a guy, but to get her mind off everything and have some fun. She might even find some inspiration for a new career.

She went to the bathroom, washed her face, and reapplied her makeup, this time using thicker eyeliner and brighter eye shadow. If she was going to have some real fun, she may as well look the part.

After pulling her hair back, she went back to her room, slid into a floral one-piece, and wrapped a knee-length turquoise beach skirt around her waist. All she needed was to find her glittery flip-flops and she would be set. It took her a minute to find them shoved in the back of the closet, then she set out, leaving a quick note for her aunt.

The band was already warming up once Maggie reached the growing crowd. Her mood lifted just being there around so many happy beachgoers. She scanned the throng of people for anyone she knew. Her gaze landed on Canyon.

Maggie's heart skipped a beat.

She didn't know why seeing him startled her. If he'd spent years traveling the world on a cruise ship, he probably loved parties and concerts.

Especially if he was the womanizer her friends said he was. Her stomach twisted in knots at the thought of it.

Why did she care? He could do what he wanted with his life. They'd been friends years ago. Now they were just strangers with nothing in common.

She shoved him from her mind and weaved her way through the crowd, finding a place with some single friends. People she needed to spend more time with.

Maggie greeted them with big hugs and before long, they were dancing and singing until the sun set, the sky offering a show of its own until the stars glittered.

Once the show was over, Maggie was exhausted from all the dancing, and it felt great. She waved to her friends, promising to hang out soon, then headed back home.

"Imagine running into you twice in one day," came a familiar voice from behind.

Maggie spun around to see Canyon. He wore long swim shorts and no shirt, showing off a perfectly tanned and sculpted torso. Her breath caught and she quickly focused on his eyes. "Well, it *is* a small town. How did it go at Figaro's?"

A funny expression shadowed his face, then he quickly smiled. "I decided not to apply. I'm going to find something here in town."

"Guess that makes two of us."

Canyon arched a brow. "Really?"

She held her breath for a moment. "I'm looking for work, too. Can't seem to find anything I really like."

"I always pictured you going to college and finding your dream career easily, then staying with it."

Maggie shrugged. "Well, I did go to college. But I still don't know what I want to do when I grow up."

He laughed. "Guess that makes two of us. I mean, I had fun on the cruise line, but it's not something I want to do for life, you know?"

"I can imagine."

"Hey, you wanna head over to Sweet Caroline's and catch up over some coffee?"

Maggie's throat was parched. "I wouldn't mind tea."

He nodded in the direction of the cafe. "Come on. My treat."

"Are you sure?"

"Yeah, I wanna hear what you've been up to."

Maggie forced a smile. "I'd rather hear about you. It sounds like you have a lot of interesting stories."

"You have no idea." They headed for the cafe, and Canyon spoke of long work hours and seven-day work weeks.

"That's exhausting just to think about."

Canyon held the door open for Maggie and she walked through.

Caroline Harper, the long-time owner of Sweet Caroline's, called out a greeting from the other end of the cafe. "I'll be right there!"

"You wanna pick a place to sit? I'll order the drinks."

"Sure." Maggie gave him a grateful smile and headed for the sofa, which an older couple was just vacating.

Maggie made herself comfortable and looked around, memories from many summers filling her mind. She'd been visiting Aunt Lucille for as long as she could remember. Auntie would bring her in when Maggie was little, then later Maggie would come in with friends. They would laugh, have fun, and often flirt with cute vacationers.

Canyon arrived with the drinks. Maggie asked about the places he'd traveled, and he told her about islands in the Caribbean, places in the Mediterranean, the majestic scenery in Alaska. If the rumors were true of him being a womanizer, he didn't mention anything about that.

It sounded like he really had seen the whole world, and it made Maggie's heart ache. She'd barely left the South her whole life. Maybe since she couldn't figure out a career, traveling could inspire her—or at least she could have some fun seeing what else the world offered.

But she would need to save some money to make that happen. Gone were the days of going on fancy vacations with her family. Not that they'd ever traveled far, having always stayed in the South.

She sighed.

"Are you okay?" Canyon's gorgeous eyes widened with concern.

Maggie's face flamed. He'd been talking, but she'd let her mind wander, and once again she was feeling sorry for herself. It was becoming a bad habit. "It just sounds so amazing to travel the world."

"You should try it sometime. Have you been on a cruise before?"

She shook her head.

"You'd love it. So, what have you been up to? I'm sure you have some stories to tell, too."

Maggie glanced behind him. "Oh, it looks like Caroline is closing up. We'd better get going."

CHAPTER 5

A bright light woke Canyon. He pulled the covers over his face.

"Rise and shine!" His mom yanked the blankets away. "If you're going to stay here, you aren't going to live like a spoiled teen. Time to find a job."

"I've been looking." He glanced over at the time. "I only got five hours sleep. I'll search again in a few hours."

"Nope. Up and at 'em. I have to get to work, and I'm not leaving until you're dressed."

Canyon started to protest, but stopped. It was useless. He'd worked tirelessly all those years, but even after quitting, he still wasn't getting a break.

"I'm getting up." His body fought him as he rose, but he was used to early mornings after much later nights.

"Good. Get dressed." She left, leaving the door wide open.

"Don't trust me, do you?" He fished some clothes from his closet and headed for the shower. The bathroom was just as small as the one on the boat.

Once he stepped into the kitchen, his mom grabbed her purse. "Tonight I want to hear all about your new job."

"Sure thing." He poured himself a cup of coffee. "Have a nice day."

"Right." She hated her job as a maid for a run-down motel outside of town. "Find yourself a job today." She left, slamming the door. The rickety walls shook in response.

Canyon sighed and sipped his coffee. If only he'd saved some of his meager earnings instead of spending them on stupid things like partying.

His stomach rumbled and he checked the cupboards. The breakfast options were a box of Corn Flakes he was sure had been there before he left to work at the cruise line, grits, or toast.

"Toast it is." He made himself some peanut butter toast and glanced around the kitchen he'd grown up in. It was hard to say if things had improved much since Dad left.

Sure, the yelling had been cut down to almost nothing and from the looks of it, nothing new had been broken. But honestly, his mom didn't seem any happier. Canyon had fled as soon as he graduated high school and his brother had done the same thing two years later, but the two had barely spoken since that day.

Maybe if Canyon could bring in some money, Mom would relax and possibly even smile. But where was he going to find work? If he couldn't find anything that day, he might have to swallow his pride and consider working for Maggie's relatives.

He finished the toast and coffee, then headed outside. It was tempting to head for the beach and take a lazy day. He could sure use one, but he really did need to pull his weight financially. Mom could barely support herself, much less him.

Canyon stepped away from his car and opted to walk around town. If he spoke with the locals, he was sure to hear about any job openings if he mentioned he was looking.

Discouragement settled in after speaking with half a dozen people, who all said they didn't know of anyone hiring. He wandered into Sweet Caroline's, hoping she might know of something. She heard all the town gossip. If she didn't know of anything, she could at least keep an ear out for him.

Caroline smiled. "Back so soon?"

Canyon nodded, unable to return the grin.

"You okay, darlin'?"

He leaned against the counter. "Just a little discouraged, Miss Caroline. Seems I came back to town at the wrong time. Nobody's hiring."

She pulled some hair behind her ear, looking deep in thought. "Yeah, everything's usually filled this deep into the season. I can give you a holler if I hear anything."

"I'd appreciate that." Canyon managed a small smile.

"It was nice seeing you with Maggie last night. I always thought you two would make a cute couple."

"Us?" Canyon gave her a double-take. "No, ma'am. We're just friends." Not only that, but they were worlds apart.

"Oh, come on. I've seen the way you two have looked at each other since you were young'uns."

"Just friends, Miss Caroline." Canyon couldn't deny his attraction to Maggie—she had always been beautiful. Now she was so gorgeous, she set his pulse on fire. The night before, he'd had to look the other way to keep from staring.

But she deserved someone much better than him, so friends they would remain.

Caroline looked like she didn't believe him. "So, is searching for work all that has you worried?"

Canyon shrugged.

"How's your mama?"

His shoulders drooped.

"That bad, huh?" She frowned.

"I'm sure she'll be happier once I find work. I don't suppose you need any help around here?"

"Sorry. I wish I did. I'd hire you in a heartbeat, sweetheart."

"Did someone say something about looking for work?" came a voice from behind.

Canyon spun around to see a familiar man about his parents' age standing there. "Uh, I'm looking."

"You a hard worker?"

"He is," Caroline interjected. "I can attest to that, Harry."

Harry glanced at Canyon and gave a nod. "I'm working on a previously abandoned house near the boardwalk. It's gonna take some serious muscle to get it fixed by the deadline."

Canyon stood tall. "I can do it."

Harry held out his hand. "Glad to hear it. When can you start?"

"Right now, if you need me."

The older man smiled. "You're a lifesaver, kid." He nodded a thanks to Caroline. "Let's have a quick informal interview, then we can get the papers signed and get to work."

Canyon followed Harry to a table in the corner and Caroline winked at him.

It was just a temporary job, but at least it was a start.

CHAPTER 6

M aggie took a deep breath as she headed down the stairs. She needed to apologize to Aunt Lucille for being short with her the night before.

Auntie was in the living room brushing Princess, her little white dog. The dog's collar matched Aunt Lucille's turquoise pumps perfectly.

"You feeling better this morning?"

Maggie stepped into the room. "I'm sorry for snapping at you last night. It was rude."

She nodded. "Do you want to talk about anything?"

"Yes, Auntie, I do." Maggie made herself comfortable on the sofa. "I'd really appreciate it if you'd stop trying to set me up with every single man in the county."

Aunt Lucille's mouth dropped. "I don't—"

Maggie cleared her throat. "I do appreciate that you care, but I'm not looking for a relationship. The last thing I need right now is a man."

"What do you need?"

"Time to find myself. What I need to focus on is building

a career. It's been a couple years, and I'm still wandering around lost. I need to figure out what I want to do."

Auntie looked deep in thought. "Do you think a place of your own would help?"

"I beg your pardon?"

"I'm sure it seems like I was never young, but I was. Like you, I had a restless period before settling down. Spending some time on my own gave me the clarity I needed."

"What are you getting at, Auntie?"

"I bought a little fixer-upper not far from the boardwalk to sell for twice what I paid. You could stay there while you figure things out, then if you want to you can rent it once you have a job."

Maggie's mouth fell open. "Really?"

Aunt Lucille sat next to her and rested her hand on Maggie's knee. "I can see that I've been suffocating you, my sweet niece. Once the little house is ready, it's yours."

Maggie's mind raced. It hardly seemed real that her aunt was not only giving her a place of her own but was also agreeing to stop playing matchmaker. "When can I start working on it?"

"Oh, no need. I hired Harry Belford."

"I'll help him." Maggie jumped from the sofa. "Let me just change my clothes."

"You don't have to. He'll be done in two shakes of a lamb's tail."

Excitement ran through Maggie. "I know I don't have to. I *want* to."

Auntie's face contorted. "You needn't do work like that. Our family hires people for things like that."

"It sounds like fun." Maggie scrambled upstairs and found some old clothes she didn't mind getting dirty. She knew nothing about painting or fixing things, but hopefully Mr. Belford wouldn't mind teaching her.

Once she was back downstairs, Auntie folded her arms and tapped her foot. "Are you sure about this?"

"Yes." Maggie stood taller.

"What are people going to think?"

Maggie grinned. "That I'm excited about having a place of my own. That I'm not afraid to get dirty."

Aunt Lucille frowned. "And that's exactly what I'm afraid people will say. Sandersons don't 'get dirty.'"

"It's a good thing I'm a Kendrick."

Auntie sighed more dramatically than a put-out teenager. "This is really what you want?"

"Yes!"

She shook her head. "Kids these days. I'll call Harry and let him know you're going to help. Just head over to the boardwalk. You can't miss the house. It has more paint chipped off than actually on it."

Maggie threw her arms around her aunt. "Thank you."

Auntie gave her a stiff hug. "I don't understand it, but you're welcome."

Maggie bounded out of the house with a bounce to her step. The afternoon sun beat down on her, but she barely noticed as she headed for the boardwalk.

The rundown home was easy to spot. Much of the gray—blue?—paint had faded and chipped off. Several windows were cracked. Branches and other debris lay sprawled across the roof and ground.

She squinted and tried to imagine the little house with some paint and love. It would be cute. Maybe Auntie would even let her paint it a shade of Maggie's favorite color, purple.

A man in his late forties or early fifties came around the little house. "Maggie?"

"Yes." She walked over and shook his hand. "You must be Mr. Belford."

"You can call me Harry. We're starting on the inside, where it needs the most work. Follow me."

They walked around the little house and up the steps to the porch. Maggie cringed, half-expecting a board to snap. None did.

The inside smelled stale and musty, despite every window being open. Sheets covered furniture. Old flowered wallpaper hung down in layers. Dust covered everything. Piles of dirt were sprawled across the scratched wood floor.

"What happened to this place?"

Harry wiped his brow. "The Alversons got too old to take care of it and moved into the Manor for their last days. None of their kids had any interest in the house, and they were more than happy to sell it to your aunt."

Sadness washed through her. The home had once been a place full of love as a family had lived there.

Footsteps sounded from the left. "Hey, Harry, do you want me to—?"

Maggie froze as her gaze locked on Canyon.

His eyes widened, mirroring the surprise she felt.

"Maggie, this is Canyon. Canyon, Maggie."

Without looking away from her, Canyon replied, "We know each other." His confused expression spoke volumes.

Maggie cleared her throat. "Aunt Lucille bought this house. I'm going to help with the cleanup."

"This is going to be Maggie's place," Harry said.

Maggie's face warmed. She hadn't wanted to mention that to Canyon.

"I see." Canyon returned to the other room.

Maggie's heart sank. Canyon probably thought she was spoiled.

CHAPTER 7

C anyon retreated to the dilapidated kitchen as humiliation ran through him. Despite trying to avoid working for Maggie's family, he'd done just that. Had he known Harry was working for Lucille Sanderson, he'd have waited for another opportunity. But he'd already texted his mom about the job, so there was no turning back.

He went back to pulling down the old wallpaper, throwing it into a pile in the middle of the floor. It would take hours to scrape off the remains before they could even think about painting.

At least that meant the job should last a while. But if Maggie was going to be here, overseeing everything, Canyon wanted to get everything done as fast as he could.

He wasn't sure how much time had passed, but by the time he finished scraping the walls, his stomach was rumbling something fierce. But he didn't have any money left for lunch. He'd spent his last few dollars on drinks at Sweet Caroline's the night before.

The smell of fried chicken filled the house.

Canyon's mouth watered. Maybe he'd be better off

finding a new job. Surely his mom would understand if this one didn't work out. Maybe there was an opening at the motel. Anything would be better than working as an underling to the prettiest and probably richest girl in town.

The food aromas made his stomach growl even worse. How was he going to make it through the day?

Maggie entered the kitchen with a smile and a big white bag. "Ready for lunch?"

"I, uh, didn't bring anything."

"This is for both of us. I thought we could take a break on the beach."

She stood in her overalls, a long braid falling over her shoulder.

He couldn't help but stare. She was beautiful even in work clothes.

"Do you want to join me?"

"Are you sure?"

"Yeah. You got my sweet tea last night. I've got lunch today."

His stomach rumbled again. There was no sense in turning her down. "I appreciate it."

They made their way to a shady spot on the beach and shared the fried chicken and potato wedges.

"I was surprised to see you today," Maggie finally said.

"Likewise." Canyon swallowed his food. "I didn't realize that house belonged to your aunt."

"She just told me about it this morning."

"I see."

They sat in silence for a few moments before Maggie met his gaze. "This is awkward."

Canyon laughed, then she did too.

"Did I do something to upset you?" Maggie asked.

Guilt stung. She was his friend, and he was acting like a prideful dog. He shook his head.

"What, then?"

Canyon grabbed a piece of chicken and took a big bite, giving him time to think of something to say that didn't make him either look pathetic or like a jerk.

He studied her and noticed a sadness in her eyes. Something he'd noticed the night before. He swallowed. "Are you okay?"

"Yeah, of course."

More awkward silence. What happened to their easy conversation the night before?

That had been before he was working for her, fixing up her house. Now the glaring differences between them were flashing like neon lights. He was from the poorest family in Indigo Bay, and she was from one of the wealthiest.

None of that had ever mattered when they were young. When they were teens, they always had something to talk about. They could sit under the stars and talk about life for hours on end with plenty more to discuss.

But they weren't teenagers anymore. The world wasn't the big place full of endless opportunities like it had once seemed. It was small and cruel, though the idealistic little town acted as somewhat of a buffer. Except that he lived in a home barely a step up from the one he was working to fix for the beauty sitting next to him.

That's when he noticed the streak of dirt across her chin and some pebbles in her braid.

Was she not acting as the overseer?

"What?" Maggie rubbed her nose. "Do I have something in my nose?"

Canyon burst out laughing. "No, and that was the last thing I expected you to say!"

"Why? Because I'm a sophisticated southern belle? Sorry to disappoint you."

They laughed again. This was what it had been like to

hang out with Maggie years before. It almost felt like no time had passed since those days.

Maggie rubbed her eyes. "I've missed this."

"So have I." Canyon stared into her bright blue eyes before his attention wandered to the sprinkling of freckles across her face, then down to her pouty lips. Bad idea. He shot his gaze back up to her eyes.

She wasn't one of the girls who threw themselves at him while on vacation. This was Maggie Kendrick, his *friend*.

The sadness returned to her eyes.

Canyon put his food down. "Are you sure you're okay?"

Her mouth curved down. "I think so."

"What's wrong?"

She sighed and played with her braid. "Life just doesn't always go the way you think it will, you know?"

"Oh, I know it. What didn't go the way you expected?"

Maggie fidgeted with her hair some more. "I was engaged. It didn't work out. At all."

The pain in her expression felt like a punch to the gut. Whoever the jerk had been, he'd really hurt Maggie. And Canyon wanted to punch the loser across the face until he was in as much pain as she was.

Canyon struggled to keep his voice gentle. "What happened?"

Maggie jumped to her feet. "I think we'd better get back to work."

"Sure." Canyon gathered the remains and put them back in the bag.

They walked back to the house in silence. A knot formed in his stomach. If only he could do something to help take away Maggie's pain.

CHAPTER 8

Maggie stared at the tiny bathroom with a surge of pride. Aside from the walls needing paint, it almost looked good as new. Nobody would ever guess it had been covered in dirt and dust that morning.

Footsteps sounded behind her.

She spun around to see Canyon climbing up the small staircase.

He stopped at the top. "Harry says we're done for the day. Tomorrow we'll—wow! Look at that bathroom. You did all that today?"

Maggie beamed. "I did. Not bad, huh?"

"It looks fantastic."

She wiped her hands on her overalls. "Who knew that cleaning was such a good stress reliever?"

"It's a workout, that's for sure." Canyon stretched his arm as if to prove the point. "I hear there's going to be another concert at the beach tonight. You want to go?"

Maggie brushed some dirt from her arm. "Sounds like fun. What time?"

"I think it's the same time as last night. Want to meet where we had lunch?"

"Sure. See you then."

Canyon gave a little nod, then disappeared down the stairs.

Maggie headed back home. Aunt Lucille was having tea with some other ladies—all true southern belles with fancy colorful dresses and perfect hair and makeup. The complete opposite of her after spending all day on the bathroom. Maggie waved to them before heading up to her room.

Once she was showered off, she felt so much better. She reclined on her bed and closed her eyes, muscles aching from the day's work. Her mind wandered to Canyon, and immediately, her pulse raced.

She couldn't help the way she felt, and her attraction to him was growing each time she saw him.

Why had she agreed to the concert? It wasn't like she had any interest in him—or any guy for that matter. No relationship had a chance. As soon as any man found out her secret, he would run for the hills.

Maybe she should just tell Canyon and get it over with. It wasn't like their friendship was going to turn into anything more, anyway. Especially if what the girls said about him held any truth. If it did, going to the concert was just one of many dates he had for the week.

Actually, he might be the perfect guy for her. If he wanted no commitment, then she wouldn't have to worry about things turning serious. They could just have some fun, and Heaven above knew she needed some of that. That alone was probably why Auntie had been so insistent on setting her up with someone. Maggie was only twenty-four, but she lived like an old maid.

Feeling lighter, Maggie bounced off the bed and found

another cute outfit similar to the one she'd worn the night before.

Downstairs, Aunt Lucille was already eating supper. Maggie joined her, giving her a big smile.

Auntie gave Maggie a funny glance. "You seem happy."

"I am." Maggie sat and piled food on her plate. "Helping with that little house was just what I needed."

"Really?" Auntie seemed confused, but then smiled. "I'm glad to hear it. How do you like the little place?"

"It's perfect, and it feels great to be able to work on it myself. I can't tell you what an accomplishment it was to transform the bathroom today."

"Sounds like you have an eye for decorating. Maybe that's something you can look into when you're ready to start a business."

"Hm." Maggie thought about it as she chewed. A little spark of excitement ignited. "That's an interesting idea. I think you might be on to something."

They made pleasant small talk until Maggie was ready to leave for the concert.

"You're going out again tonight?" Auntie appeared pleased.

"I am. I might not be able to move a muscle come morning, but it'll be worth it."

Aunt Lucille gave her a quick hug. "Have fun, little miss."

Maggie practically skipped out the door. Everything seemed to be turning around, and now she even had a direction to start focusing on when she was ready to think about her career.

When she got to the lunch spot, Canyon was already there. He was leaning against a tree, looking deep in thought.

Maggie bounded over to him, but he didn't notice. She tapped his shoulders. "Boo!"

He jumped and turned to her, his eyes wide.

She burst out laughing. "You're still so easy to scare!"

Canyon chuckled and shook his head. "And you haven't changed a bit. You used to love sneaking up on me."

"Because you made it so easy." She gave him a playful shove. It was so easy to fall back into old ways around him, and she'd really missed the lighthearted summer days spent with her old friend.

"Guess I do. My brother used to like scaring me, too."

Maggie burst out laughing, suddenly remembering a long-forgotten memory. "Do you remember the time your brother and I teamed up and surprised you behind the library?"

"The slime incident of my sophomore year! It took me a full day to get stuff completely washed out."

They laughed until Maggie's stomach hurt. It felt so good to enjoy herself so freely. It had been way too long.

Canyon regained his composure first. "Want to head over to the concert? We can still get a good spot."

She caught her breath. "Yeah, let's."

To her surprise, Canyon took her hand in his and they walked across the sand to the stage. Maggie kind of liked it.

People were starting to arrive, but there were still plenty of good places. Canyon led her to one near the front. They made small talk with some of the other beachgoers until the first song began.

The music matched Maggie's good mood, and she danced like she never had before.

Canyon gave her a smile that made her stomach tingle a little, then he showed off his moves. Whereas Maggie was rusty, he danced like it was second nature.

Not only that, but he looked great as he danced. His smile lit up his face, and her eyes kept roaming to his muscles as they flexed naturally.

She pulled her attention away from him and focused on

her own dance style. With as much fun as she was having, it was easy to shake off the rustiness and dance like she'd never stopped.

Canyon arched a brow and upped his game with moves she'd never seen. He'd probably learned them somewhere exotic.

That wasn't going to deter her. Maggie had a good imagination and used to hold dance-offs with her friends on the weekends. She had plenty of lesser-known moves herself.

People around Canyon and Maggie gave them space, and soon started cheering them on.

Beads of sweat broke out around her hairline and dripped into her face. She barely took the time to wipe them away as she swung her arms and legs to the tune of the music.

The song ended, and people clapped and whistled. More were looking at her and Canyon than the band. She should've felt bad but didn't. Her only thought was beating her world-traveling friend.

Before she had time to catch her breath, the next song began.

"You ready for more?" Canyon's eyes held a dare.

"More? That was just a warmup! I haven't even *started* yet, pretty boy."

He threw his head back and laughed, then they both jumped into motion, moving along with the beat.

Others called out their names. People were choosing sides. It was officially a competition.

After the fourth song, Maggie was ready to drop from exhaustion, but pride kept her going. Canyon hadn't even broken a sweat. He'd probably danced every night for the last seven years.

Maggie wasn't going to let him win. She could rest later, even if it required alternating hot and cold packs all over her body. Between the crowd's excitement and the looks Canyon kept giving her, she had enough energy to draw from to keep her going all night if needed.

Eventually, the band announced they were about to play their last song. That was the best news Maggie had heard since she'd started dancing. She would definitely spend the next day lying around, unable to move. But for now, she had one more dance.

She tilted her head at Canyon. "You ready to give up?"

"Me? Never!"

"Good." Maggie put everything she had into the last song of the night. Her feet ached, her legs throbbed, her arms hurt —basically everything with a muscle cried out in pain.

Once the song was over, people crowded around them, giving high-fives and congratulations.

CHAPTER 9

Canyon grinned at Maggie while they were surrounded by the audience they'd attracted. She gave him her bright smile in return.

That girl had some serious moves. He'd danced all over the world but had never seen anyone like her.

It made her all the more alluring. It also shattered all his preconceived notions about her. Maybe she wasn't the sweet, innocent southern girl he'd always thought her to be.

And those looks she kept throwing his way as they danced the night away… His heart sped up just thinking about them. Maybe the two of them stood a chance at something more than just friendship.

That was something he'd always wanted but never dared to hope for. Though they'd been good friends, Maggie had always been way out of his league—even before his father left the family poor and struggling.

When the crowd thinned, Canyon made his way over and put his arm around her. "Where've you been hiding those moves?"

"Just been waiting for the right time to bring them out."

"I'm impressed."

She beamed. "Really?"

"Yeah. So was everyone else."

Maggie shrugged. "I was just having fun. It wasn't like I was trying to show off or anything." The shine in her eyes told him she was totally teasing.

"Sure, okay." Canyon stepped back and stared into her eyes. The desire to place his lips on hers overwhelmed him. It took everything in him not to. He cleared his throat. "You wanna walk along the water? I know you're not tired, but I wouldn't mind soaking my feet."

Maggie gave him a playful smirk. "Sure, if that's what you want."

He took her hand again and threaded his fingers between hers. They headed for the water and he kept his attention focused on that, because if he looked at her, he wasn't sure he could keep his mouth to himself.

They removed their shoes and walked along the shore, the waves lapping over their ankles.

Canyon wanted to stop walking, pull her close, and kiss her. He'd ignored his feelings for her for a lifetime. After dancing and now holding hands, all those desires were exploding to the surface.

Maggie was the one girl he'd always wanted, but never thought he would have a chance with. Yet here she was, walking along the bay with him, her soft hand in his.

One thing was for sure—she was far different from all the other girls. He'd had one fling after another for all those years because he was trying to get his mind off the one he couldn't have.

Now that he actually stood a chance, he needed to tread carefully. He would treat her like gold and deny his every desire to win her over by showing her how special she was. Maggie Kendrick deserved nothing short of his best.

She turned to him, breaking his thoughts. "This is really nice."

Canyon squeezed her hand. "It really is."

They walked for a while, then turned and headed back toward their shoes. His heart ached at the thought of having to let go of her hand, to go their separate ways.

He had work early in the morning but didn't care. The only thing he wanted was to drink in more time with Maggie.

His mind raced as they headed for their sandals. He needed an excuse to stay there with her.

"Where did you learn to dance like that?" he asked.

"Just with my friends growing up." She didn't ask about his moves.

"In Georgia?"

Maggie sat and wiped sand from her feet. "Yeah."

Canyon plunked down next to her, barely leaving an inch between them. "I was going to say, I don't remember you dancing when you spent your summers here. I'd definitely remember that."

She glanced at him and smiled.

His pulse raced again. She had an effect on him that nobody else did. "It's nice to see you so happy again."

Maggie tilted her head. "What do you mean?"

"You seemed so sad before. Like you had the weight of the world on your shoulders."

She frowned, a little of the sadness returning to her eyes. "I suppose I did."

Canyon wanted to kick himself for ruining her joy.

"When my engagement was broken, it felt like the end of the world." She drew in a deep breath and looked up at the moon. "Like something was wrong with me."

"What?" He cupped her chin and guided her to look at him. "There's nothing wrong with you. Nothing at all.

41

Don't let anything that jerk said make you think less of yourself."

She studied him but said nothing.

"I've known you forever. I speak as an expert."

Maggie gave him a sad smile, then her eyes shone with tears.

Canyon's throat closed up. He might break if she cried. "What is it?"

She blinked and a single tear ran down her face. "Actually, there is something wrong with me."

He clenched his jaw. If her ex-fiancé were right there, Canyon would punch him into the next week. "I told you, no there isn't."

Maggie swallowed. "I can't have kids. Nobody's going to want to marry me."

"Are you kidding me? Any man would be lucky to marry you."

Another tear ran down her face and her beautiful lips trembled. "But I can never give a husband a child of his own."

"There's a thing called adoption, you know."

More tears spilled onto her cheeks.

Canyon's heart raced. Some jerk had broken her heart because she couldn't give him kids? That was it? He'd been that close to marrying the most wonderful woman alive, and he'd treated her like she was nothing?

A range of emotions ran through him—anger at the loser who'd hurt her, pain for her heartache, and the desire that had been growing for her since he was just a kid.

Maggie's mouth continued trembling as more tears fell.

Canyon couldn't just sit there while she cried. He had to do something. He leaned closer to her and wiped a tear from her face.

She glanced up at him, a single teardrop clinging to her lashes.

Her pain overwhelmed him. He moved closer and kissed a tear away.

Maggie didn't pull away. In fact, she didn't move at all.

Canyon trailed kisses along the path of her tears until he reached the corner of her mouth. His heart pounded like he was a fourteen-year-old who had never kissed a girl.

He'd never kissed *this* girl before. The woman of his dreams, who had always been out of his reach.

She didn't pull away, so he moved his lips to hers. They were so soft and sweet. She returned the kiss and put her hands on his bare arms. His skin tingled at her touch as though he'd gone his whole life without ever grazing hands with another.

CHAPTER 10

Maggie closed her eyes and relaxed, finding healing in Canyon's kisses. His words rang through her mind.

Nothing was wrong with her. And his kind, gentle kisses seemed to prove the point further.

His touch was nothing like Dan's had been. When Dan had kissed her, it had been rough. Harsh. Like he owned her rather than treasured her.

Now in Canyon's arms, kissing him, Maggie felt valued. It was crazy, though, because they weren't even romantically involved. Or were they now?

She shoved aside all thoughts and just enjoyed the moment. Canyon's arms tightened around her, pulling her even closer.

Maggie breathed in his scent—he smelled like the salty sea air—and enjoyed the sweet, soft kisses.

He opened his mouth, and with it hers.

Her eyes flew open. This was happening too fast. It shouldn't be happening at all. She wasn't doing relationships or anything that came with them.

Maggie pulled away, gasping for air.

Canyon opened his eyes. "I'm sorry. I shouldn't have done that."

"No, I… It's just too fast."

He took a deep breath and a range of expressions crossed his face. "I know. That's why I'm sorry. It just hurt me to think about all the pain you're in."

Maggie's heart skipped a beat. He actually cared about her heartache that much?

"I won't do that again, Mags. I promise."

She leaned against his shoulder. "It's okay. Really."

He wrapped his arm around her and kissed the top of her head. "How long ago did that happen?"

"It's been a couple years." She drew in a deep breath. "I should be over it by now."

"It's hard to just get over something painful. Believe me, I know."

Maggie nodded but wasn't entirely sure what he was referring to. Was it his dad's abandonment, or something else altogether?

They sat in silence for a while, watching the lazy lapping of the water onto the shore.

It felt good to be sitting there with Canyon, especially with his arm around her. He offered protection and comfort, things she hadn't realized she'd needed so desperately.

But could they continue down this path as friends? The way he'd kissed her made her think there was more than just friendship behind it all. Or had he just gotten caught up in the moment, overcome by her grief? It was possible. They'd always been good friends growing up, in tune with what the other was feeling.

She yawned.

Canyon turned to her. "I should get you home."

Maggie wanted to protest, but she was too tired. Her muscles were aching even more than they had been while dancing. Not only that, but her eyelids were growing heavy. Despite her desire to remain in his arms, she nodded. He was right. She needed to get some sleep.

He helped her up and she slid on her flip-flops. Once Canyon had on his sandals, he put his arm around her again and they strolled across the beach and over to her aunt's house.

On the porch, he kissed her forehead. "Have sweet dreams."

Maggie wanted him to brush her lips with his, for him to kiss her again like he did at the beach. Instead, she gave him a tired smile. "Thanks, Canyon. You too."

His gaze lingered for a few moments before he spun around and headed away.

Sighing, Maggie unlocked the door and stepped inside. When she was about to close the door, she noticed Canyon watching from the street.

He was making sure she got in safely!

Dan had never done that. He'd always driven away as soon as she was out of the car.

Maggie gave a little wave before closing the door. She locked it, then leaned against it and let out a sigh.

What a night it had been. Not only the dancing, but that kiss… It had been the things fairy tales were made of. That was the kind of thing she'd dreamed about since she was a little girl, but she'd learned to assume didn't exist in real life. At least, not for her.

She cleared her throat. It probably still didn't exist for her —not for long, anyway. A relationship wasn't in her future. Nothing serious, at least. But maybe she could have fun with Canyon for a while.

He knew her secret—that she couldn't have kids—so it wouldn't be like she was hiding anything from him. She wouldn't be offering him any false hope of a real relationship.

Maybe she could just enjoy the time with him, then for the rest of her life hold onto memories like the night she'd just experienced. Maggie was sure she would never forget that kiss. She'd certainly never forget how wonderful it felt to be treated with such care and gentleness.

Thank goodness for a great friend giving her something like that to hold onto and treasure.

She tiptoed upstairs, not wanting to wake Aunt Lucille who was surely sleeping at this late hour.

As Maggie got ready for bed, then finally climbed in, aching and sore, her mind kept replaying the entire evening. The dancing, the competition, the feel of her hand in his, and of course that kiss.

With any luck, there would be more times like that over the summer. More wonderful memories for her to hold onto once they both figured out what they wanted to do with their lives. For now, she would take a season of reliving her childhood summers. Maybe this one would be even more enjoyable.

She drifted off to sleep with a smile on her face and her heart full.

CHAPTER 11

C anyon barely heard his alarm but managed to pull himself out of his dream to hit snooze. Then he rolled over and buried his face into the pillow, wanting another five hours of sleep.

It took a moment to remember why he was so tired. He'd been out dancing and talking with Maggie.

His heart raced at the thought of kissing her. It was something he'd dreamed about since he was twelve or thirteen when he'd realized how wonderful she was, but even then he'd known better than to pursue her.

So why now? What was different? He was actually worse now than before with all those years of wild living—nightly parties and never spending more than a week with any one girl.

Guilt stung, making his stomach twist. Sweet, innocent Maggie had opened up to him, but would she have if she had realized what he was really like?

He'd find out at work. Just the thought of seeing her in less than an hour was enough to pull him out of his sleep stupor and make him jump out of bed.

Canyon turned off the alarm and got ready with a hum on his lips. It was a tune he'd learned on an island somewhere. Jamaica? Grand Cayman? It was so hard to remember for sure.

His mom gave him a funny look as he entered the kitchen. She finished pouring her coffee. "What has you in such a good mood?"

He didn't feel like talking about Maggie yet. "I've got a job."

"And yet you stayed out until the wee hours last night?"

She still knew how to squash someone's good mood. "Yeah, I did. I'm used to it, and I'll be fine."

"I'm going to need you to pick up some groceries tonight."

"I don't have any money yet. It's gonna be two weeks until I see a paycheck."

"That hasn't stopped you from eating my food."

He sighed. "I should have another payment from the cruise line coming in soon, but I doubt it'll be today."

"Well, figure something out. There's nothing for dinner and I just paid rent." She headed out the door. That was when Canyon noticed she looked as tired as he felt.

"Hey, Mom. Are you okay?"

"Fine. Just gotta get to work." She left without another word.

Canyon frowned. He looked through the cupboards and the fridge. Just some cereal, crackers, ketchup, OJ, half a block of cheese, and some frozen vegetables.

He was going to need to think of something. A second job? Maybe he could borrow some money from a friend.

Canyon was nothing if not resourceful. Maybe he could get a dinner shift at a restaurant and bring home some food for his mom. It wasn't ideal, but it was doable.

He poured himself a cup of coffee and downed it quickly

before heading out. Before long, his mind had wandered from money troubles back to Maggie. At least she didn't have to worry about food or paychecks as the grand-niece of Lucille Sanderson.

Canyon greeted Harry at the house and got to work pulling old tiles from the kitchen floor. Time went by quickly despite his rumbling stomach. Coffee wasn't the most filling breakfast.

By the time Harry declared their lunch break, Canyon was famished. His only real option was cheese and crackers at home. Maybe some frozen peas, if they weren't older than he was.

Canyon walked through each room of the house, looking for Maggie.

He stopped Harry as he was heading out the door. "Did Maggie come in today?"

Harry shook his head. "Haven't heard from her or Lucille."

"Thanks." Canyon waved and plopped down on a dusty couch.

Was Maggie just tired? Or was she having second thoughts about the night before? Did she regret kissing him? Or telling him about not being able to have kids?

He pulled out his phone to call her when he noticed a missed text. It was from his friend Javier from the cruise line.

Javier: Hey man. Finally paid you back to your PayPal.

Canyon raked his mind, trying to remember what Javier owed him. It must've been an old debt because Canyon couldn't remember.

He logged into his account, and sure enough he had a balance of two hundred and fifty dollars. That would buy more than groceries!

He texted a quick thanks to Javier, then headed to Sweet Caroline's for a sandwich and an iced coffee.

Another text came in as he was walking.

Javier: Don't thank me. Everyone who helped with that service project for the orphans just got a bonus.

Canyon: Really? Sweet!

He checked his bank account real quick, and he had another two-fifty in there. Five hundred dollars!

It was his lucky day. Canyon's mind raced as he ate his food by the cafe window and watched tourists and locals alike wandering up and down the street outside.

After practically inhaling the food, he pulled out his phone to call Maggie and see how she was doing when the phone rang in his hand. It was Archer.

"What's up?" Canyon greeted his friend.

"You're in Indigo Bay, right?"

"Yeah. Why?"

"I've got a week off, and I'm just a couple of hours away. Time to party! And we just got those bonuses. Best timing ever, dude."

"Can't, man. Sorry."

"What?" Archer practically yelled in his ear. "I met these two totally hot twins. Twins! They're from like France or something. Blonde and accents. Get your butt over here."

"Like I said, I can't."

"Are you crazy?" Archer exclaimed. "Didn't you hear what I said?"

Canyon held Maggie's face in his mind. "I'm seeing someone."

"Like you have a date for tonight already? Dude, reschedule. I'll send you a picture."

"No, I mean there's someone special in my life. I'm not dropping her for some random chick. Plus, I have a job here in town."

Archer sighed dramatically. "Who sucked all the fun out of you? Fine, I'll call Damon. Last chance."

"Have fun, Archer." Canyon ended the call and took a deep breath. He was more than happy to leave that life behind if it meant spending time with Maggie. And now he had some money. He could take her somewhere nice, even after buying his mom groceries. Maybe he could even get a haircut and a new shirt.

CHAPTER 12

M aggie kicked her foot up, sending a rippling wave through the rainbow-colored bath water. The bath bomb had done more than just tint the water, it was actually helping her sore muscles.

She couldn't remember the last time her body ached so much. Not that she regretted all the dancing. She'd never had more fun, and she couldn't stop thinking about Canyon—his smile, his dance moves, his muscles, and the kiss. Especially the kiss.

Her pulse raced every time that memory surfaced.

Part of her wanted to head over to the house just to see him, but she had no energy to do any work. Not when she could barely lift her arms or legs. One of the retired folks with walkers at the Manor could outrun her today.

No, she needed to take care of her aches today so she could get some work done tomorrow. But who was she kidding? Ninety-five percent of the reason she wanted to go to the little house—her future home—was to see Canyon.

Maggie sighed deeply, closed her eyes, and slunk down under the colorful water. She stayed there until her lungs couldn't take another moment, then she sat up and drew in a deep breath.

Her phone rang, but it was just out of reach. She dried her hands on a towel then pulled herself up and grabbed it just as it stopped ringing. The screen showed a missed call from Isabella.

Did she want to talk about her enormous engagement ring again? The girl could talk about the ring and her new fiancé for hours on end.

Maybe it was for the best that she'd missed the call. On the other hand, with Canyon on her mind all day, talking about love suddenly didn't seem like such a depressing topic.

She unlocked the screen and returned the missed call.

"What are you doing right now?" Isabella greeted her.

"Enjoying a bath."

"Want to meet me somewhere? I've got to get out of the house. I'm going stir crazy!"

Maggie poked her toe out of the water, making it ripple again. "Sure. What do you have in mind?"

"Anything. We can go back to the beach, we can chat over iced tea at Sweet Caroline's, or whatever you feel like. I need some girl time, Maggie." She begged with her eyes.

"Tea sounds great." And sitting definitely sounded better than walking around in the sweltering heat of the late afternoon. "Meet you in an hour?"

"Can't wait!" Isabella made a kissing sound, then ended the call.

Maggie put her phone down, then closed her eyes and enjoyed the last few minutes of her bath before pulling the plug with her toes.

Once the water drained, she got ready twice as slowly as usual thanks to her still-aching muscles.

By the time she made it to Sweet Caroline's, Isabella

already sat at the couch with two iced teas. She waved Maggie over and handed one of the drinks to her.

"Thanks." Maggie plopped down and drank half the glass without stopping.

"Thirsty much?" Isabella teased. She pulled a tablet from her handbag and slid her finger around the screen until a wedding dress popped up on the screen. "What do you think of this one?"

Maggie leaned forward and studied the flowing dress that sparkled with what had to be thousands of sequins. "It's gorgeous."

"It isn't too much?"

"Can anything on a wedding day be overdone?"

Isabella squealed. "I think I'm going to get this one! I just wanted confirmation. Mama said it was way too much."

Maggie zoomed in on the dress, studying it from every side. "I think it's perfect."

Isabella wrapped her arms around Maggie. "Thank you! That's exactly what I thought, too. Mama's just too old-fashioned to understand today's brides."

Maggie nodded, but instead of picturing Isabella in the dress, her mind conjured a picture of herself in it.

"Now about the flowers…"

Maggie's mind wandered as her friend talked about her wedding plans.

"…Don't you think?"

Maggie turned to Isabella. "Say that again?"

"This bouquet is okay for a winter wedding, right?"

"You're getting married in the winter?" Maggie asked. "Indigo Bay is perfect for summer weddings. Spring, even."

Isabella sighed. "Have you heard a thing I've said?"

Maggie's cheeks warmed. "I've been trying to listen. It's just—"

"Oh my gosh! You're thinking about a guy, aren't you?"

Isabella's expression lit up. "Who is it? Is it serious? We all totally thought you were still hung up on what's-his-face."

Maggie frowned. "Dan."

"Oh, I know. I just didn't want to say his name." Isabella put her hand on Maggie's knee. "So, who's the guy taking up your thoughts?"

"It doesn't matter." Maggie picked up her glass and sipped the water from the melting ice cubes.

"How can you say that?" Isabella put down her tablet. "You've been moping forever. Who's the guy?"

"I'm never marrying, so seriously, it doesn't matter."

"Never marrying? Because of Dan?" Isabella made a disgusted face. "Don't let that jerk take up anymore of your headspace. You're beautiful and sweet. He's a mindless pig who doesn't know what he lost."

"Thanks, but it isn't so much him as it is me."

Isabella's brows knit together. "What do you mean?"

Maggie tapped the side of her glass. "I'm just not marriage material, that's all."

"You?" Isabella shook her head. "That's crazy. I can see you as one of those moms with a whole gaggle of kids. Children adore you."

"Can we get back to talking about your wedding?"

"Sure, but seriously, forget about Dan and whatever he said to you. You're wonderful, and you'll have the perfect family someday."

Maggie grabbed the tablet from Isabella and asked her a question about the floral arrangement on the screen.

Isabella's eyes widened, and she spoke about it, apparently having forgotten all about Maggie's love life—or lack of it. Canyon was nothing more than a friend, and neither of them were marriage material.

CHAPTER 13

C anyon stared at the full fridge before closing the door. His mom was sure going to be surprised when she got home.

He scarfed down a couple more pieces of the pizza he'd picked up and closed the box to keep it as warm as possible until she got home. Then he checked his phone for Maggie's number, and gave her a call.

"Hello?" asked a gruff, unhappy voice at the other end.

Canyon arched a brow. "Uh, is Maggie there?"

"Who?"

"Maggie."

"Ain't no Maggie here." The call ended.

Apparently she'd changed her number since high school.

Canyon sighed. Now what?

Lucille's number wasn't in his contact list, either. Nor were any of Maggie's friends.

He wasn't going to sit around wondering if Maggie was upset about the night before. Not when they were in a small town and he could easily find her.

Canyon climbed into his car and headed over to Lucille's

house. Driving by the enormous well-manicured homes, his beat-up car stuck out like blood on a white shirt.

He held his head high and parked along the curb, then marched up to the Sanderson house and knocked.

Footsteps clacked from the inside. They sounded like high heels. Probably Lucille, as Maggie was more of a flip-flop kind of girl.

The door flung open, and a wave of strong perfume hit Canyon before he saw the older woman in a flowered dress and heavy makeup. "Yes?"

He cleared his throat. "Evening, Miss Lucille. Is Maggie around?"

She raised her nose at him and narrowed her eyes. "And you're asking, why?"

"Because I'm looking for her, ma'am."

Lucille tapped her heel on the hardwood floor. "Is this regarding her house?"

"No. I'd just like to see her."

"Sorry. I can't say where she might've gone."

Disappointment washed through Canyon, but he wasn't about to let Lucille see that. He stood taller. "Thanks, anyway. Have a nice night."

"Mm-hm. Why don't you head back home, then? Good-night." She closed the door between them.

He glared at the door before spinning around back to his car.

Maggie wasn't among the crowd of people waiting for the evening's concert. She hadn't stopped by the house to work on it. He checked a few more places, but she wasn't at any of them either.

Maybe she was at Lucille's, but her aunt wasn't going to let him in to find out. But there was no way to know, and he wanted to see her, so he would just keep looking.

Canyon checked several popular places around town and

some lesser-known ones. Maggie wasn't at any of them, and he'd built up quite a thirst.

He parked near Sweet Caroline's and went into the busy cafe for an iced drink. He didn't really care what after all his running around. He got in line and glanced at the choices.

Caroline greeted him with a wide smile. "How are you doing, Canyon? Did things work out with Harry?"

"Yes, I'm working for him on a house. Thank you very much, Miss Caroline."

"I'm glad to hear it worked out. Now, what can I get you?"

"Something cold and refreshing. Care to surprise me?"

"Sure thing." She bustled around behind the counter, talking about an upcoming fair in a nearby town. Then she handed him what looked like regular tea and told him the total. "It isn't what you think. Let me know how you like it."

Canyon gave a quick nod, then handed her exact change. "Thanks, darlin'."

He went over to the only empty table in the place and sat so that he could see out the window, just in case Maggie happened to walk by. He took a sip of the drink—Caroline had been right. It wasn't what he was expecting.

It was so fizzy, it tickled his nose. And it had a really tart fruit taste. But it was cold and refreshing, and that was all he cared about.

Canyon stayed there, sipping the drink and studying the people who walked by outside.

Then he heard a familiar laugh. It sounded just like Maggie.

He spun around and glanced around the cafe.

His heart skipped a beat.

Maggie stood in front of the couch, laughing with Isabella Price.

Canyon scrambled out of his chair and did his best to stroll over like it was no big deal. Like he hadn't just spent over an hour looking for her before finally giving up. "Maggie."

She turned his way and her expression lit up. "Canyon!"

Relief washed through him. She was happy to see him— that meant she hadn't been avoiding him because of the kiss or their discussion the night before.

Isabella, however, frowned and folded her arms. "What are you doing here, Leblanc?"

"Oh, the last name. What did I do to offend you?"

Isabella's entire face contorted with disgust, then she pulled Maggie toward her and whispered.

It was like they were in grade school again. Except Maggie hadn't looked like that fifteen years earlier.

Canyon cleared his throat. "Do you want to go to the beach again, Maggie?"

Isabella glared at him, then stepped back from Maggie but kept her gaze on her. "Daisy Nash is having a game night. Lots of people. You guys should go. I'd go, but I'm helping out my grandma in about an hour."

Canyon struggled to keep his posture relaxed. Isabella was obviously suggesting the game night to keep Canyon from being alone with her friend. As though Canyon were a snake ready to strike, or as if Maggie were incapable of making her own decisions.

Maggie glanced at him. "What do you think?"

"I'm up for whatever you'd like to do. It might be fun to catch up with everyone." And hopefully show people that he wasn't as bad as people clearly thought he was, given the reactions he'd been garnering since his return.

"As long as it doesn't involve walking or dancing, it sounds great. I'm a little sore from last night."

"I'm not surprised. You danced up a storm for hours."

Isabella scowled and gathered her things before turning back to Maggie. "Want me to drop you off at Daisy's?"

"We can take my car," Canyon offered.

Isabella's brows knit together.

Maggie smiled. "I'll just go with Canyon, but thanks. Have fun with your grandma."

"I can drop you off. It's on the way."

Canyon shook his head in disbelief. People really didn't think he was good enough for Maggie.

He'd show them.

CHAPTER 14

M aggie waved to Isabella, trying to ignore her thundering heart. Canyon stood just inches from her, and Maggie's cheeks warmed just thinking about their kiss.

Canyon chuckled. "That was fun."

Guilt prickled. She'd been hoping Canyon hadn't noticed Isabella's disdain, but of course he had. "Sorry about her. She just, uh…" Maggie tried to think of a polite way to say her friend didn't like him and definitely didn't want Maggie around him.

Canyon put his hand on her bare shoulder. It was a simple gesture but sent a wave of excitement through her.

"Don't feel like you have to defend her to me." He nodded to the left. "I'm parked this way."

They headed toward the car in silence. Maggie wanted him to hold her hand, but he didn't. Isabella must've scared him off.

She stared at his hand, wanting to grab it, but not able to get her own hand to budge from her side.

Canyon stopped walking, and she crashed into him.

"Are you okay?" he asked.

"Yeah, sorry." Her face flamed. She wasn't one to blush so easily, but since he'd walked back into her life, it felt like she was doing it constantly.

"This is my ride." He pointed to a rusty sedan. "It isn't pretty, but it'll spare us walking all over Indigo Bay."

She forced a smile, her face still warm. "Sounds good to me."

He unlocked the passenger door and held it open for her, closing the door once she was seated inside.

As Maggie buckled herself in, Isabella's warnings ran through her mind. "He's not the kid you used to know. Canyon's a player—he goes through women faster than you or I change our shoes. If the rumors are true, he's had more girlfriends than the population of Indigo Bay."

While Maggie appreciated her friend's concern, she didn't believe the rumors. They were clearly exaggerated—there was no way Canyon had had that many girlfriends.

Her stomach twisted at the thought. She didn't want to think of him with anyone else, much less many someones.

Canyon sat in the driver's seat and started the car. "Does Daisy still live at the same house?"

"Yeah, her parents gave it to her and moved to a place closer to the water."

Maggie studied him as he pulled into traffic—which meant all of five other cars. Canyon slid on a pair of dark sunglasses and tapped his fingers on the steering wheel in time with the music. He was so sure of himself, not caring what people thought of him.

Her heart fluttered. She wished she could be so confident, especially in the face of people who thought less of her.

After Dan had dumped her, long-time friends and family started giving Maggie the same looks Isabella was giving to Canyon. People acted like there was something wrong with

Maggie—and there was, but there wasn't anything she could do about it. Dan wanted kids carrying his DNA, and she couldn't give that to him.

There wasn't just something wrong with her. She was defective.

Tears stung her eyes and she blinked them away.

No. She wasn't defective. Dan was the one who had something wrong with him. He was an arrogant jerk who thought the world owed him.

In reality, he'd have been lucky to marry her. She had been a devoted girlfriend, and she would have been even more so as a wife.

"Are you okay?" Canyon's voice broke through her thoughts.

"What?"

"You just sighed like you have the weight of the world on your shoulders."

Maggie shrugged. "Just thinking. That's all."

"Anything I can help with?"

Kiss me like you did last night.

She cleared her throat. "No, but thanks."

"Okay. Looks like we're here." Canyon pulled over and parked behind a line of cars. He opened Maggie's door for her again, then they walked a block down the residential road until they reached the Nash home.

Music and laughter could be heard from the driveway. A group of people were gathered in the front yard, playing horseshoes.

Canyon and Maggie waved to them as they made their way up the walkway. The door was unlocked, so they went in, and again Canyon held it for her.

Laughter sounded from various directions. They wandered through some rooms, greeting partygoers. There were several card and board games going in a few rooms. A group of guys were playing Twister in the living room near some others who were deeply involved with a video game.

Canyon turned to Maggie. "What would you like to do?"

"Anything other than Twister. I hurt just watching them."

"Hey, Maggie!" Daisy waved from a table in the dining room. "Come and join the game."

She glanced at Canyon. "You want to?"

"Sure."

They headed over to a card table that was filled with a board game and colorful pretend money.

"Monopoly?" Canyon asked.

"Pokémon Monopoly," Daisy corrected. "Cate and Dawson are leaving. You two take their places."

Cate pulled some red hair behind her ear. "Sorry, I'm losing."

"I'll take your place, then." Canyon held out Dawson's chair for Maggie. "Why Pokémon Monopoly?"

Daisy laughed. "Because that's the only version I have around here. Obviously, it's old."

"Oh? I thought you bought it yesterday." Canyon scooted Maggie in, then sat next to her.

"Always the kidder." Daisy laughed again, and then the game got underway.

Maggie studied her cards and money, trying to figure out how well she was set up. It looked like Dawson had racked up some pretty decent properties.

Everyone continued laughing and having a good time. Maggie discovered she was in the lead and managed to hold her position. Canyon quickly went from losing to beating half the people around the table.

Just after passing Go once again, his hand brushed hers. Maggie's breath hitched. Canyon glanced at her and gave a quick grin. Her heart skipped a beat, but she managed to return the smile.

As they continued playing, Canyon brushed her hand and arm several more times.

After a while, Daisy landed on one of Maggie's properties and gave all her money to Maggie. "That's all I have. I'm out. I think I'll make nachos."

"Then Charades?" Ella asked.

"Whatever everyone wants!" Daisy bounced over to the fridge and pulled out a bunch of nacho toppings.

Ella landed on one of Canyon's properties. "I'm out, too."

Canyon nudged Maggie. "They're dropping like flies. Looks like it might be between you and me. Think you can beat me?"

"Sure do. Hope you don't mind losing to a girl."

"My ego can take it, but luckily it won't have to." He winked and placed his hand on top of hers.

A warm tingle ran up her arm. If he kept doing that, she wouldn't be able to concentrate long enough to stay in first place.

CHAPTER 15

Canyon stared at his pile of money, then Maggie's. It was about equal, and it had been at least half an hour since anyone else had been in the game. "Call it a tie?"

She tapped her chin, looking deep in thought. Then she locked her gaze on his. "I kind of wanted to see you lose to a girl."

The sparkle in her eyes fired a spark in him. He'd move any mountain to give her what she wanted. "Is that really what you want?"

Maggie nodded, the corners of her mouth twitching.

"Okay." Canyon scooped up all his money and cards and dumped them in her lap. He rose and bowed to her. "Maggie is the reigning champion! I bow to her greatness."

She laughed, with a slight pink coloring her cheeks, then she emptied the contents of her lap and curtsied. "Thank you, kind sir."

Canyon held out his hand, and she placed hers on top. He threaded his fingers through hers. They walked through the house, checking out the other games. The wild game of Twister was still going, but now with onlookers chanting.

Several board and card games were in full swing in various rooms and there was a competitive round of Charades taking up one room.

"What do you think?" Maggie asked.

He studied her full lips, wanting to kiss them. It took all his effort to pull his gaze to her eyes. "What do you want to do?"

"We could see if anything's going on out back."

"Sounds good to me."

They made their way to the back door and found the backyard empty. Little Tiki torches lit a path that led to a reflection pond.

Canyon squeezed Maggie's hand and led her to the walkway. They walked slowly. It took a few moments for his ears to stop ringing from the sudden quiet.

"This is nice." Maggie gave him her dazzling smile.

His heart jumped into his throat. He nodded, unable to find his voice until she turned to look at the pond. "It really is."

They stopped walking once they reached it. She leaned against him and stared at the water.

Canyon put his arm around her. "I've really been enjoying my time with you."

"So have I." She drew in a deep breath. "I haven't told anyone around here about why Dan left me. Not even Aunt Lucille knows the reason."

His heart broke for her, knowing how much it had to have hurt her. "Have you told anyone else?"

She didn't answer right away. "No. I was going to tell my parents and sister after Dan, but after he broke up with me, it was too much to deal with all at once. Then I decided I'm never going to marry, so the kid thing became irrelevant."

"You really shouldn't let that stop you from getting

married—if that's what you really want. Any man worth his salt would love you regardless."

Maggie shrugged.

"You don't believe me?"

She didn't answer.

Canyon turned to her, placed his hands on her shoulders, and held her gaze. "I'm serious, Maggie. You're beautiful and smart, and a whole lot of fun. Any guy would be lucky to be with you."

Her eyes misted. "That's really nice of you, but—"

"But nothing. I mean it. Any man would be proud to be with you. Your ex? He's a complete idiot."

Maggie's eyes widened, then before he realized what was happening, she pressed her soft, sweet mouth on his. Once he realized she was kissing him, he pulled her closer and took in her sweet scent and the feel of her in his arms.

He wanted to hold onto everything about the moment in his memory. There was something about Maggie that made a simple kiss feel monumental. It made his pulse catch fire and his breath hitch. One sweet kiss was more thrilling than anything else he'd ever experienced.

If he could go back in time and erase the past seven years, he'd do it in a heartbeat.

He rested one hand on the small of her back and kept the other on her arm, making sure to keep himself in full control.

Maggie pulled back and stared into his eyes. "Thank you."

In reply, he placed his lips back on hers and dipped her slightly. She tightened her fingers around his arms, and he flexed a little. Then he stood up straight and held her gaze, getting lost in her blue eyes—they seemed brighter than before.

Canyon took her hand again and led her over to a tree, and they sat at the base. His mind raced, thought after thought vying to be the one spoken, but he let the silence between them say everything.

Maggie leaned her head against his shoulder and rested her hand on his knee.

Again, the small innocent gesture sent a wave of excitement through him. Being with her was like sweeping him back to a time before he'd ever kissed a girl. Everything was new and special.

She was new and special.

He played with a ringlet of her hair. "Everything I said earlier was true."

"You're too good to be true."

Canyon laughed. "Me?"

"Yes, you." There was a smile to her tone.

"I'm pretty sure you're the only person to think that."

"Well, you're the only one who has bothered to find out *why* my engagement fell to pieces. Everyone else just wants to fix me—push me to forget about it."

"I'd be lying if I said I didn't want you to forget about him, but I get that you have to heal from what he did to you."

"See? You're perfect."

He kissed her temple. "If you keep saying that, I'm going to start to believe it."

"Good." She squeezed his knee.

Canyon took a deep breath and held it before letting go. "There are rumors running around town about me."

"I know."

His heart pounded. "Do you know what they are?"

She nodded. "I've heard them, Canyon."

"Which ones?"

A beat of silence. It felt like an eternity.

"That you were a womanizer."

His stomach clenched hearing from her mouth, but he

liked how she put it in the past tense. He swallowed. "The rumors are true, Maggie."

She turned and stared into his eyes, her expression inquisitive and maybe a little hurt, but without any judgment.

It pained him to hold her gaze. "If I could take it all back, I would. If I had ever thought I had a chance with you, I never would have made the choices I did. Not that I think I deserve a chance with you."

Maggie bit her lower lip.

Canyon drew in a deep breath and held it. If she knew what that did to him, she would turn bright red. "Say something."

She shifted her position. "You've always had a chance with me. I waited so long for you to make the first move."

He gave her a double-take. "You did?"

Maggie gave a little nod. "I didn't have the nerve to when we were younger. You were a year older and had lots of girls interested in you. I understood why you never saw me as anything more than a friend."

Her words felt like a slap to the face. He needed to tell her how he felt, but it might scare her off. Maybe he should keep his feelings to himself. But she looked so conflicted. He needed to tell her. He took a deep breath. "You were the first person I fell in love with, Magnolia Lucille Kendrick."

"Wh-what? You were in love with me?"

"Madly."

Somehow her eyes managed to widen even more. "Why didn't you ever say anything?"

He took her hand and ran his thumb across her palm. "You were way out of my league. I wanted to at least have you as a friend rather than risk losing you altogether."

"Oh, Canyon." Her words seemed to hold finality to them.

As though it was too late for anything to come of their love now.

"I'm sorry, Maggie. For everything—for being too chicken as a teen and for everything else I've done since then to ruin what we could've had."

CHAPTER 16

M aggie's heart thundered as she stared at Canyon and processed everything he'd said. He had been in *love* with her and had never said anything.

Canyon Leblanc had been in love with her.

With her.

It hardly seemed possible.

Oh, how things would have turned out differently if only she'd known. If he hadn't run off and started working for the cruise line. If she'd had the chance to give things a try with him those years ago.

But now everything was different. She couldn't allow herself to even consider a serious relationship. He might think that her inability to have kids wasn't a big deal *now*, but he'd surely change his mind later. He deserved to have kids with his own genetics, and that was what mattered in the long run.

It was something she couldn't give him, or anyone. All things considered, it was probably for the best that he'd never told her his true feelings all that time ago. Then it might've been him she'd disappointed when the doctor gave her the news.

Canyon cupped her chin. "What are you thinking?"

"I… I'm just processing everything."

"Tell me this. What would you have done if I'd have told you how I felt back then?"

She swallowed, her pulse picking up speed. "I'd have been thrilled."

"What if I told you my feelings have picked up where they left off and grown since the moment I saw you?"

Her breath hitched. She stared into his eyes, anchoring herself. "I'd say that would explain the kisses."

Canyon tilted her chin closer to him, leaving only about an inch between their mouths. "What about you?"

"Me?"

"How do you feel now? About me?"

Maggie's heart felt like it would explode out of her chest. She struggled to breathe normally. What was she supposed to say? There was no denying her feelings for him—they were stronger than they'd ever been for Dan.

In fact, if she was being completely honest with herself, her long-ignored love for Canyon had been a bigger problem for her and Dan than the doctor's news. That just made them see all their problems for what they really were, even though she hadn't thought of Canyon in so long.

"Maggie?" Canyon's voice was practically a whisper. His eyes held an intensity that took her breath away. "Should I assume that your kisses also say more than words ever could?"

Without blinking, she gave a little nod.

His mouth gaped. "You… you feel the same way?"

"Yes, Canyon. I always thought you were too cool to like me like that. I was just happy being your friend, running around town all summer every year, telling each other everything."

"Not everything," he corrected.

"Right."

Silence settled between them as they stared into each other's eyes. Finally, Canyon spoke. "You really thought I was cool? Too cool to date?"

Her cheeks warmed. "I never thought I stood a chance. I figured you would want to be with someone more… I don't know. Pretty. Popular. Funny. More athletic."

"We were both idiots."

She tilted her head, questioning.

"I don't mean you're an actual idiot. It's just that, how do I say this? Who on earth could be prettier than you? You're not only gorgeous, but the best friend a guy could ask for. And you're both funny and athletic. Popular? Honestly, I never paid much attention to that stuff. All year long, I counted down the days until summer. Not because of being out of school, though that was nice. It was *you*. I had to see you in person, not just pictures online. Chatting over social media was never enough."

Maggie's limbs went weak. It was a good thing she was already sitting. She really had been an idiot.

Canyon rubbed her cheek with his thumb. "What about now? How do you feel now?"

"Too much." She leaned against him, falling against his chest.

He wrapped his arms around her and held her tightly.

Maggie's mind raced. She hadn't been expecting any of this. It had just been a spur-of-the-moment decision to go to a local game night.

Everything Canyon had said threatened to crush her. She could hardly process it, much less make any sense of what it meant for them now. For the future.

Her time with Canyon was just supposed to be a fun summer fling. Replaying times long gone with an old friend. But now it was so much more.

There was no going back from this conversation.

She couldn't un-hear his declaration of love for her. Not just love, but a lifetime of longing.

Regret squeezed her. All those wasted years. If only one of them had opened up, things could've gone so differently.

Canyon rubbed circles on her back. "Are you okay, Mags?"

Was she? Would she ever be again? What was she supposed to do now?

He kissed the top of her head. "Will you tell me what you're thinking? Let's not make the same mistakes again."

She drew in a deep breath, then sat up straight and looked into his eyes. "I don't know what to think, other than that things could've been so different."

Canyon took her hand in his. "I know. I'm so sorry. Does my past put you off?"

The question stung. "I'd be lying if I said it doesn't hurt to think about you being with so many others."

His face fell. "More than anything, I wish I could take that back. If I had ever thought I had a chance with you..." His voice trailed off and he sighed before looking back at her. "Just know that I would never do anything to hurt you. You're the only one I care about—the only one I've *ever* cared about."

Tears stung her eyes. "You're the only one, too."

He squeezed her knee. "It's okay that you loved your ex. I can't hold that against you, and I don't. I never should've left town without first telling you how I felt. Without giving us a chance."

She bit her lip. "But I didn't love him like I should have. I see that now. He lashed out at me because I think he knew he never really had my heart."

Canyon's brows came together. "What do you mean by 'he lashed out at you'? Did he hurt you?"

"No! That was a bad choice of words. I just meant that he broke up with me. That's all."

He sat up taller, his nostrils flaring. "Did he hurt you?"

Maggie shook her head.

"Are you sure?"

"Yes."

"Why would you say that, then? That he lashed out at you?"

She took a deep breath, overcome by his protective nature. "I just—he was mad at me. That's all. He never hit me. I swear."

Canyon's mouth formed a straight line. "Mad at you? Because you couldn't give him kids? What kind of monster is he? He should've been grateful you wanted to spend your life with him! That's more than enough—more than anyone could ask for."

"Things were complicated. Like I said, I didn't realize I hadn't fully moved on from you. He knew he didn't have my whole heart. I always held back part of it from him. The medical report, it just brought everything to light."

Canyon pulled on his hair. "You swear he never hurt you?"

"Yes."

"Okay, because if I ever find out he did, I can't guarantee my actions."

"He didn't, so you don't have to worry about that." Maggie's heart thundered. She hadn't expected him to react so strongly. Nobody had ever been that concerned over her well-being before.

Canyon pulled her into his embrace and they clung to each other wordlessly.

CHAPTER 17

C anyon took another sip of his double-strong espresso. It wasn't helping—not when he was this tired. But he hadn't been able to bring himself to take Maggie home any earlier than he had the night before.

That conversation had taken him by storm. He hadn't expected to open up to her like that. He'd never laid himself bare like that to anyone, ever. But it had all been for the best. It still hardly seemed real that Maggie had admitted to having feelings for him going back as long as he'd loved her.

He still wasn't entirely convinced her ex-fiancé hadn't been harsh with her, but Canyon had to take Maggie at her word. If she said he hadn't, he would believe her until there was further proof of his instincts being right. They usually were, but maybe this time they weren't because of his over-powering emotions for her.

"You taking a break?" Harry's voice brought Canyon back to the present.

He set the drink on the kitchen counter. "Just tryin' to wake up."

"It's almost noon." Harry wiped his brow. "I had to take

out the pipes in the bathroom. Gonna have to replace those this afternoon, then I need to check the ones down here. It's going to take longer than I anticipated."

"I can take a look before lunch."

"You know how?"

Canyon wiped his brow. "Sure. Dad taught my brother and me about plumbing when we were kids."

"Well, okay. Maybe you should take a nap instead of eating. We've got a lot to do this afternoon."

A nap did sound good. Canyon rolled up his sleeves and opened the doors underneath the sink. "I'll be on the top of my game after lunch."

"Better be." Harry left the room.

Canyon maneuvered himself under the sink and used his cell phone as a flashlight to check the pipes.

Footsteps sounded a few minutes later.

"These ones look good," Canyon called before sliding out from under the sink.

Maggie stood there, holding a white plastic bag. She wore a bright pink sundress, and from Canyon's angle, he could see more of her legs than she would've felt comfortable with.

He quickly averted his gaze and scrambled to his feet, wiping sweat from his forehead. "Sorry, I thought you were Harry."

"No worries. I get that a lot." She grinned, obviously teasing.

Canyon burst out laughing. "Right. It's great to see you. What's in the bag?"

"Chinese takeout. You still like that, don't you?"

Did she remember that had been his favorite? "I love it. Let me just wash up."

After he cleaned the dust and dirt from his hands and face, they headed for the beach.

Canyon took the bag from her and slid his fingers

between hers. "It was really sweet of you to pick this up."

She beamed. "It was the least I could do after keeping you out late two nights in a row."

"Or maybe I kept *you* out."

Maggie laughed, then they made themselves comfortable at the same spot they'd eaten at before. It was quickly becoming their spot.

She held up forks and chopsticks. "Which do you want?"

"Chopsticks, of course." He grinned and took a pair.

"That's what I thought. I got plates, or we can just eat out of the containers like we used to."

"Who needs plates?" Canyon pulled the chopsticks from their little sleeve and held them like a pro—he'd been using them for as long as he could remember.

She set down the other pair. "I've never been any good at those. I'll stick with a fork."

"Want me to help you with them?" He liked the thought of wrapping his hand around hers to help her get the right hold.

Maggie shook her head. "You tried before, remember?"

He did, and he also recalled how badly he'd wanted to kiss her with her so close. "That was years ago. I'm sure you can do it now."

She bit her lip and appeared to be considering it.

He wanted to be the one biting that lip.

Maggie looked back at him. "Maybe next time. It could take all day, and you have to be back at work soon."

Disappointment washed through him until he realized that was the perfect excuse to get together again soon. "So, it's a date?"

She grinned. "It's a date."

They dug into the food, their hands constantly bumping against each other as they shared the sesame chicken, chow mein noodles, and fried rice.

The hour for his lunch break flew by too fast. It was over

before it barely started.

Canyon gathered the empty containers into the bag, then took both of Maggie's hands into his. "Thanks so much for lunch. It was the perfect surprise."

She smiled. "I'm so glad."

"So, are you going to come back and help with the house again? Or have you decided against it?

"No way. It's going to be my place. I want to work on it. If only I could get to sleep early enough." Her eyes sparkled.

Canyon cupped her chin and brushed his lips against hers. "I'll have to give a stern talking-to to the guy who's been keeping you up."

The corners of her mouth twitched. "I'd like to see that."

"I'll give him a smack down he won't soon forget." Canyon gave her another kiss, this time letting his lips linger a moment longer.

She rubbed the scruff on his cheek. "If you keep this up, I'm going to have a hard time letting you go back."

He wrapped an arm around her. "That doesn't sound so bad to me."

"I don't want to get you fired."

"Aren't you technically the boss?"

"Aunt Lucille is."

Canyon flashed back to the stink-eye Lucille had given him when he'd been looking for Maggie. "True. I probably shouldn't give her a reason to dislike me."

Maggie held his gaze. "I'll be waiting for the date where you teach me how to use chopsticks."

"How does dinner sound?"

"You want to eat Chinese two meals in a row?"

"It's my favorite—just after you."

She grinned again. "It's a date, then."

Canyon drew in a deep breath. How had he gotten so lucky?

CHAPTER 18

Maggie leaned against the tree and watched Canyon until he was out of sight. She sighed and let her mind replay every moment of the lunch, including the brief kisses.

"What was that?"

Maggie turned toward the voice.

Isabella stood in front of her, hands on her hips.

"What was what?"

"You and Canyon." Isabella tilted her head.

Maggie sighed, more from reliving the lunch than from her annoyance with her friend. "It was me and Canyon enjoying lunch together."

"You don't believe me? The stuff I told you?"

"He's a changed man. That's why he's back in Indigo Bay."

Isabella made a clicking noise as she shook her head. "Guys like that, they don't change. Not really."

"What's that supposed to mean?" Maggie stared her down.

"He's going to use you. I hate to say it, but as we speak, you're probably one of many."

Anger churned in her stomach. "No, I'm not! He works all day, then we spend some time together until it's way too late, then he gets only a few hours of sleep before he heads back to work. I even spend his lunch with him. I don't know why I'm explaining this to you. I'm an adult, and I can see who I want."

Isabella rested her hand on Maggie's arm. "I'm worried about you. You've always adored him, even though you never would admit it. He's going to hurt you, and I don't want to see that happen to my friend."

Maggie scowled.

"Hey, I get it. Bad guys are hot. There's something about them that draws us to them. But it's better to fall for a fictional baddie than to flirt with one in real life."

Maggie clenched her jaw. "He's not going to hurt me."

"Have you seen *Reign*? There are some serious baddies in that show. Henry, Narcisse, Bash…" Isabella took a deep breath and fanned herself. "Talk about some hot fictional boyfriends. We can watch that together, then find you a real-life good guy. Trust me, that's what you actually want."

"I don't want a fictional boyfriend or some random nice guy. The only person I have any interest in is Canyon. I'm sorry if you don't like him, but that doesn't change how I feel."

"Oh, honey. I know how you feel. Really, I do. Remember my fling with Travis Conley? It was fun until Bridgett Lawson and I found out he was seeing both of us."

Maggie scowled. "I'm not you, and Canyon isn't Travis. I appreciate your concern, but it's unwarranted. Why don't you focus on your wedding?"

"Why are you so determined to wind up hurt?"

Maggie stared Isabella down. "I love him! I've always loved him. He's the real reason my engagement fell apart. We've both made mistakes. Neither of us is perfect. But now that we know how we feel about each other, I'm not about to walk away from that. Maybe it won't work out, and you can gloat all you want. But it's not going to end until I've given it everything I have. Then do you know what I'll do?"

"I'd never gloat over your unhappiness."

Maggie ignored the statement. "If it doesn't work out with Canyon, then I'm done with men. It's him or nothing! If you can't support me, then please just leave me alone."

Isabella's mouth dropped.

Tears blurring her vision, Maggie spun around and stormed away.

"Maggie!"

She didn't turn around. While she did appreciate the concern, her friend needed to learn to keep it to herself.

Maggie didn't slow as she made her way home. She didn't even make eye contact with anyone or give any friendly hellos. People might complain to Aunt Lucille, then she would have a chat with Maggie about her rudeness, but Maggie didn't care.

Once inside the house, she nearly crashed into her auntie.

"Maggie!"

"I need to be alone right now."

Aunt Lucille stepped between Maggie and the staircase. "What has gotten into you lately? You're acting like a hormonal teenager. I've been patient, but it needs to stop."

Maggie took a deep breath. Anything she said was likely to only prove her aunt's point.

"What's going on? Is there something I can help you with?"

Maggie relaxed, but didn't feel like talking about Canyon with her.

"Does it have anything to do with that Leblanc fellow?"

How did she know?

"Several people have said they've seen you around town, holding hands and acting like a couple."

Maggie gritted her teeth.

"Are the rumors true?"

"What if they are?"

Aunt Lucille frowned, and many of the lines around her eyes and mouth deepened. "His family is less than reputable. That mother of his is divorced and has never remarried. And from what I hear, Canyon's worse than her, finding a new plaything each night on the cruise line."

Maggie's anger from before bubbled over, threatening to explode. She bit her tongue, not trusting her mouth. She took a deep breath, trying to find something to say that would calm the situation.

Aunt Lucille stepped forward. "I forbid you from seeing him again."

"What?" The room spun around Maggie. "You can't do that! I'm an adult."

"You're also living under my roof. And if you want that to continue, you need to stay away from him. If you walk into Sweet Caroline's and he's in there, you turn around and go somewhere else."

Anger like Maggie had never before felt raged through her. She took a deep breath. "Tell me one thing. Are you serious?"

The look on her face answered the question.

There was so much Maggie wanted to say, but none of it would help. She raced past her aunt and up the stairs to her room, feeling helpless like a child. At twenty-four, she was being told who to date!

Her aunt had a surprise coming if she thought she could control Maggie like that. Especially now. Yes, Maggie was living under her roof and eating her food, but that was because she was practically a second mother. That didn't change the fact that Maggie was an adult.

Why did everyone think they knew better than her? Even Isabella, who was supposed to be her friend, was trying to mother Maggie. Why did they think she was incapable of making a decision for herself?

She paced her room, occasionally stopping at the window and staring at the ocean. What she needed was a plan to figure out a way to live on her own. That was the problem—she was still living like a child. She needed to take on more responsibility so people would look at her seriously.

The first thing she needed was to get a job, maybe two. Whatever it would take to build up enough savings for first and last month's rent somewhere. Maybe one of the cottages that Dallas, Caroline's son, owned and rented out. She was pretty sure those came furnished. That would certainly help. Or maybe she could rent a room or an apartment. There had to be *something* available, even in the height of tourist season. Even if she didn't have anything other than her clothes, at least she would be on her own.

CHAPTER 19

C anyon glanced at his phone again. Maggie had texted him that she'd meet him at the restaurant fifteen minutes earlier, but she still wasn't there.

He was about to call her when he saw her running across the street.

She ran inside, out of breath. "Sorry I'm late. I was… Well, I lost track of time."

Canyon wrapped his arms around her. "It's okay. I was beginning to worry, but I'm just glad you're fine."

Maggie returned the embrace, then stepped back. "I had to run a couple errands, and one of them took longer than I expected."

"No problem. Is everything all right?"

"Yeah. I'm ready to eat."

"That makes two of us." Canyon turned to the server, and she led them to a booth. Canyon scooted in next to Maggie. "You ready to learn how to use chopsticks?"

She gave him a determined smile. "I was born ready."

He laughed, then they looked over the menus.

Maggie fidgeted, tapping the table and twisting her hair around a finger so tightly that it turned white.

"Sure you're good?"

"Of course." She didn't look up from the menu.

Canyon rubbed his chin. Something was definitely up, but he wasn't sure that pushing the subject would help. He wanted to help, but she didn't seem to want any.

Maybe she would decide to open up after a meal. He was famished, and maybe she was too, if she hadn't eaten since their lunch together.

The silence between them remained until they ordered the food. Then Canyon took a deep breath and put an arm around her. She didn't lean against him like other times.

He cleared his throat. "Harry and I are making good progress on the house. It's going to look like a whole new place when we're done with it."

"Oh."

Oh? That was all the response he got from that? Canyon studied her. She was still strangling her finger with her hair and her brows were knitted together.

"Something on your mind?"

She frowned. "Sorry. I'm not being much of a date, am I?"

He squeezed her shoulder. "I'm happy to be here with you no matter your mood. If a quiet meal is what you need, we can reschedule the chopsticks lesson."

Maggie turned to him, tears shining in her eyes.

Canyon's heart dropped to his stomach. Had he said something wrong? "Maggie, I—"

"You're the only one who understands me."

"I am?"

She nodded and wiped at her eyes. "This has been the worst day."

"Why? What happened?"

Maggie leaned against him, and he ran his hand over the length of her hair. She sighed deeply. "It was going great up until we had lunch. I had so much fun, but then as soon as you left, I ran into one of my friends and we got into an argument."

"About what?"

"You." Maggie took a deep breath.

"She doesn't think I'm good enough for you?"

Maggie sat up and held his gaze.

"It's okay," Canyon assured her. "You can say it. I know how people feel about me around here."

Her expression softened, then she frowned again a fire burning in her eyes. "I *hate* that people see you that way."

Her intensity caught him off guard. "It's my own fault. I chose to come back home after living a life that ninety-nine percent of the locals disagree with. Most of the rest of the world has moved on and isn't so old-fashioned. I'm okay with it—I just don't want anyone giving you a hard time."

The food came, and they ate quietly, Canyon with the chopsticks and Maggie with a fork.

His mind raced, trying to think of something to say that would fix everything. But there was nothing he could say or do. He'd made his choices, and now he had to live with the consequences. Unfortunately, that also meant that Maggie had to deal with them, too.

He turned to her. "For what it's worth, I'm sorry you're getting grief over me. I can talk with Isabella if you want me to."

Her eyes widened. "I never mentioned Isabella's name."

Canyon wiped his mouth with the napkin. "She made it pretty obvious she doesn't want us together."

Maggie's shoulders slumped. "Yeah, it was her. They think they're protecting me."

"They?"

"I got into a fight with Aunt Lucille right after arguing with Isabella."

It all made sense all of a sudden—Maggie's mood. Isabella and Lucille were the two people who were the most judgmental of Canyon, and Maggie'd had to deal with both of them since lunch.

"What can I do?" he asked.

"I don't suppose you know of anything for rent?"

He arched an eyebrow.

"And I do mean anything—a room, a cottage, an apartment."

"What about the little house Harry and I are working on?"

Maggie's expression tightened. "I'm getting out from under Aunt Lucille's thumb."

"Meaning?"

"I'm an adult. It's time I start acting like it."

Canyon held her hand and rubbed his thumb on the inside of her wrist. "Does this have to do with me again? You were so excited about that little place."

She looked away. "I need to stop leaning on my family. I'm almost twenty-five."

"You didn't answer my question."

Maggie's expression tightened. "Yes. Okay? She forbade me from seeing you again. If I'm going to see you, it can't be while I'm living under her roof."

"Oh, Maggie. Why didn't you tell me?"

"I didn't want you to feel bad."

"What about how you feel?"

"I'll manage."

Canyon slid his fingers through hers. "Do you think she'll really kick you out? Maybe I should give you space while you decide what you're going to do."

She stared into his eyes, the fire returning. "I don't want space, and I don't care if she does give me the boot. In fact,

I'd like to see that. I'll move into your place, and see how she likes that."

"You don't mean that."

"I do."

He kissed her nose. "I know that's the anger talking. And besides, I won't have you move in with me. People will really talk then."

"I don't care anymore. They can say what they want."

Canyon shook his head. "How about this? We'll keep seeing each other, but not out in public. Your aunt probably has people watching to see what you're doing around town. Once we've got you settled into a rental, we can walk around town all we want."

She frowned. "You want to sneak around? We don't have anything to hide—nothing to be ashamed about!"

"We don't, but think about it this way. It's kind of exciting. It'll add a dose of spice to every date we go on."

Maggie pursed her lips, clearly not convinced.

"It won't be forever. Just until we get you settled somewhere on your own. Maybe by then, people's opinion of me will improve after they've seen me going to work every day. They'll also have to notice that I'm not living wildly. Then people won't feel the need to protect you."

She folded her arms. "Innocent, naive Maggie who can't think for herself."

"People don't see you like that."

Maggie lifted a brow.

"I don't." He sat taller. "Who cares what anyone else thinks?"

She sat up straight, too. "Yeah. Who cares about them?"

He kissed her palm. "Where do you want to go for our first top-secret date?"

CHAPTER 20

M aggie held her head high and walked into Guest Services at the cottages. Her stomach twisted in knots, but she ignored it. She needed to find out if there were any rentals available and also if there were any job openings. Chances were low for both this time of year, but there was only one way to find out for sure.

Zoe glanced up from the reception desk and gave her a wide smile. "Hi, Maggie. What brings you in here?"

"Hi, Zoe. I have two quick questions."

"Lay them on me."

Maggie's heart pounded. "Are there any cottages for rent?"

"Right now? Or later? I think we're booked solid for a while."

"Anything."

Zoe turned to her computer and clicked on the keyboard. "Nothing until after Labor Day."

Disappointment washed through Maggie, but she didn't let her smile fade. "Thanks for checking. My other question is if there are any job openings."

Surprise registered on her face. "Are you looking?"

"Keeping my options open."

"Other than Jace wanting another assistant handyman— or woman—I don't think so." She typed at the computer again, then turned back to Maggie. "Do you want me to check with him, or maybe Dallas?"

"Um, sure. Thanks, Zoe. Can you call me on my cell phone? You don't need to call me at my aunt's house."

"Sure thing." Zoe slid her a piece of paper.

Maggie scrawled her number down. "Thanks again."

"Sure thing. Anything else I can help with?"

"That's all. Have a nice day."

Zoe smiled and held up a plate of sticky buns. "Want one for the road?"

Maggie's stomach rumbled. She'd skipped breakfast, wanting to avoid Aunt Lucille. She picked one up and her mouth watered. "Thanks!"

"No problem." Zoe turned back to her computer.

Maggie hurried out of the building, her cheeks burning. She didn't think that being an assistant handyman was beneath her, but it wasn't what she'd pictured herself doing. She'd thought Zoe might need an assistant or perhaps take her place if she was going to be taking some time off.

It was also her fifth no for a place to live for the morning. If things didn't improve, she would end up renting something outside Indigo Bay. That might be for the best, actually. None of her neighbors would care who she dated.

Maggie pulled out her phone and went to her note app. The next on her list was the Happy Paws Pet Shop. It wasn't far away, between the cottages and city park beach.

Before she reached the door, Maggie could see Sterling Montgomery inside, painting a kitten on the store's window.

"Hey there, Maggie," he greeted her.

"Hi." She gave a little wave.

"Can I help you with anything? We just got a litter of kittens in. They're sweet little things."

Maggie forced a grin. "Actually, I was wondering if you have any job openings."

"I wish we had your old position to offer you, but one of the teens filled it for the summer."

"That's okay. Just thought I'd check."

"Did I hear someone ask about a job?" Violet appeared, pulling her long hair into a ponytail. "Oh, hi, Maggie. Are you looking for work?"

Maggie nodded. "I am."

"We don't have anything, but my cousin Cassidy is in town for a convention. She was saying she could really use some help."

"With what, exactly?" Maggie tried to ignore the prick of excitement budding.

"She runs a doggie daycare and hotel back in Enchantment Bay, Oregon, and she's getting ideas to improve her business. There are too many classes for her to attend by herself, so she's looking for someone who can go to some of those and take notes."

"Doesn't she also need some help with bookkeeping and notes?" Sterling called.

Violet nodded. "I think she does. Are you interested?"

Maggie nodded. "How long does she need help?"

"It's only a week, but she really wishes she had someone to assist her. She'll pay top dollar. We'll also give you a glowing referral since you were such a great employee for us."

"I have a business degree. When can I meet her?" Maggie asked.

Violet glanced at the clock. "Wonderful! She should be in here in about an hour or two—she didn't get any sleep on her red-eye flight last night."

"Can you send me a text when, I mean if, she wants to meet me?"

"Sure." Violet smiled. "And I know she will. You still have the same number?"

Maggie nodded. "Thanks so much!"

They said their goodbyes as she headed out the door. She wasn't sure what Violet meant by top dollar, but it certainly had to help.

Maggie was so excited, she headed over to the little house. Inside, she found Canyon sanding cupboards in the kitchen.

He glanced around as he climbed off the step stool. "You shouldn't be here. Harry could come downstairs at any moment—he works for Lucille, if you've forgotten."

"Let him see us together." Maggie kissed him, then sneezed from the dust on his face.

Canyon wiped his brow. "I thought we were going to sneak around?"

"I have a job. Well, probably. And it's only a week, but it's a job. I can look for something more permanent during my breaks."

Footsteps sounded down the stairs.

Canyon pulled Maggie aside, opened the door to the pantry, and waved her in.

"Are you serious?"

"Hurry!"

Maggie glared at him but stepped inside. Canyon closed the door, and a moment later, she could hear the muffled conversation between him and Harry.

It sounded like Harry wanted to work on the cabinets with Canyon.

Maggie groaned and leaned against a shelf. It was dusty and stuffy in there, and she wanted to get home to freshen up before meeting Cassidy. She couldn't show up covered in dust.

After a minute, Maggie shifted her weight. The shelf popped loose and sprung up before crashing back to where it started.

She spun around and reached for it, but the noise had already been made.

Harry said something in the kitchen, sounding startled.

Canyon responded. It sounded like he said something about mice.

Maggie put her hands over her face and shook her head. If Harry opened the pantry door, it would be a lot worse for her than if she'd just been in the kitchen.

He would tell Aunt Lucille about this for sure.

She felt around for a light switch and found none. So she jumped to position, pretending to work on the broken shelf.

A minute later, the doorknob wiggled.

Her pulse raced, drumming in her ears. She fought to keep her breathing steady and she forced a smile, trying to think up an excuse that didn't sound completely stupid.

The door creaked as it opened slowly.

She moved the loose shelf up and down, trying to look like she was doing something useful. Inside a dark pantry.

Light blinded her. Once her eyes adjusted, she saw Canyon standing there.

"What are you doing?" The corners of his mouth twitched.

She glanced behind him to see where Harry was. She spoke as loudly as she could without yelling. "Just trying to fix this shelf. You know, like you asked me to."

Canyon chuckled. "Harry just left to get some rat traps."

"Sorry."

"Don't be. Otherwise I couldn't do this." He stepped into the pantry, pulled her close, and kissed her.

Maggie's heart raced, and she was breathless by the time he stepped back.

Canyon grinned. "That was kind of fun. I actually like this sneaking around." He scooped her up and kissed her again. "Don't you?"

"It does have a certain appeal." Even if it did make her feel like a teenager again. Maybe that was part of why she loved it.

CHAPTER 21

Maggie leaped out of the shower, conditioner still on her hair, and reached for her ringing phone without checking her caller ID. It could only be one of two people, and she didn't want to miss a call from either Violet or Canyon.

"Hello?"

"Maggie, it's me," said the all-too-familiar male voice at the other end of the line. "Don't hang up."

She nearly dropped the phone, and not because of her slippery hands. "What do you want, Dan?"

And why hadn't she blocked his number?

"I have something important to tell you, but it can't be over the phone."

Her stomach lurched. She never thought she'd have to speak with her now-engaged ex-fiancé again. "I don't want to see you. Just tell me what it is."

"Didn't you hear me?" He sounded annoyed. "I told you, it's too important to say over the phone."

She stared at the growing puddle pooling under her as if it would tell her what to say to get Dan off the phone.

99

"Are you still there? Maggie?"

"I'm here, but I need to get going. Tell me, or don't. I need to get going. I have an appointment to get to."

"Can you come here?"

"Have you lost your mind?" Maggie exclaimed. "No, I can't. I have important things to do, and I'm not dropping any of them to drive to Georgia. Much less to see you."

He sighed, something he only did when highly irritated. "Okay, then. I'll come to you."

"Really, you don't have to."

"Where are you? It's noisy in the background."

"Near a waterfall." She wasn't about to admit she had stepped out of the shower to talk to him.

"They have waterfalls at Indigo Bay?"

"I'm hanging up now."

"Are you still staying with your aunt?"

"Bye, Dan." She ended the call and set the phone down before climbing back into the shower.

The phone rang again as soon as she started to rinse the conditioner out. She stayed put. No way she was talking to Dan again, and she also couldn't talk to anyone else right then. He'd managed to completely sour her mood.

She sprayed some aromatherapy mist and breathed in the relaxing aroma, holding it until she felt a little better. Then she repeated the process until she was in the right mindset to head over to the pet store and meet Violet's cousin.

Dan kept popping back into her mind, but she pushed him away. She'd finally managed to move on, and he decided to reappear in her life? Did he have some kind of radar detector or something?

Stop!

Maggie left the house through the back door and avoided Aunt Lucille. Maybe she'd feel like talking to her again once she had a permanent job lined up. Maybe.

She made her way to the pet store, greeting people along the way.

Once she entered the Happy Paws Pet Shop, Sterling waved from his place painting the window. "Cassidy's back in the office."

"Thanks!" Maggie's pulse raced, but she ignored it as she headed into the area for employees only.

A tall, pretty woman with long black hair and bangs sat at Violet's desk, typing away on a laptop.

Maggie cleared her throat. "Hello. Are you Cassidy?"

The lady glanced up, nodded, and smiled. "I am. You must be Maggie?"

"Yes. Nice to meet you." Maggie shook her hand, then sat on the other side of the desk.

Cassidy pushed the laptop to the side and held Maggie's gaze. "Violet says you were wonderful to work with when you worked here."

"I'm a hard worker, and I put everything into whatever I do."

"You understand the pet business?"

Maggie nodded. "I learned a lot working here."

"Why did you leave?"

"Business slowed after tourist season." Maggie had also decided that wasn't the job she wanted as a career, but she didn't need to mention that to Cassidy, did she? Especially not for a job that was only going to last a week.

They discussed the details of the upcoming pet convention and what exactly she needed from Maggie. Cassidy then glanced back at the computer screen. "Tell me about your work history."

Great. Ever since Maggie had been back at Indigo Bay, she'd had a trail of unrelated short-term jobs. Maggie shifted in her seat. "I have a business degree and—"

"You do?" Cassidy's eyes widened, hopefully with excitement.

"Yes. I just haven't found the right job to apply it toward yet."

"This is perfect." Cassidy smiled, putting Maggie at ease. "I'm struggling with my books. Believe me, business is not my strong suit. You'd probably take one look at my records and laugh at me. I started my doggie daycare and hotel because of my love for pets. Crunching numbers and dealing with red tape had nothing to do with it, yet that seems to be about half of what I deal with. I thought hiring a receptionist would help, but that's not what she does. None of them has been a help in that department."

Maggie leaned back in her chair. "I'd be happy to take a look, if you'd like."

"You're a lifesaver." She reached down and grabbed a large bag, then rifled through it, finally pulling out a manila envelope. "If you could just fill out this paperwork first, then I can show you my mess and see if you can make any sense of it."

"I'm sure it isn't that bad." She took the papers from Cassidy and began filling them out while Cassidy turned back to her laptop.

A few minutes later, Maggie's phone rang.

"Sorry. I forgot to put that on silent."

"No problem." Cassidy smiled, then turned back to her computer.

Maggie dug her phone out of her handbag to silence it but froze when she saw the screen. It was Dan again. She turned the ringer off and made a mental note to block his number—something she should've done long ago and couldn't do while she was at the end of a job interview.

Once she had the paperwork filled out, Maggie handed it back to Cassidy, who looked it over, nodding. "I'm so glad to have you on board. Do you promise not to laugh when you see my books?"

"Of course I won't laugh."

"Well, I won't blame you if you do. Come on over here and let me explain my methods. I have a feeling it's probably nothing you ever saw in business school."

Maggie got up and went around to the other side of the desk. At least her new boss was as friendly as her cousin. It would make the next week a lot more pleasant.

CHAPTER 22

Canyon's stomach rumbled as he walked away from the house after a long day's work. The highlight of the day had been seeing Maggie, and that hadn't lasted nearly long enough.

He wanted to eat but had one more thing on his mind that was more urgent than food—talking to Isabella.

It was one thing that Maggie's aunt was against them being together—there wasn't much he could do against someone so influential in town—but he *could* have a face-to-face with Maggie's friend.

The girl had always been a beach bunny, so that was the first place Canyon headed. And sure enough, she was sprawled out on a towel with some other locals.

He marched over and cleared his throat. All three glanced over at him.

"What do you want?" Courtney asked. She looked like she could go into labor at any moment.

"I want to have a word with Isabella."

"Can't you see I'm busy?" Isabella pulled her sunglasses down over her eyes and rolled to her stomach.

"She's busy. Go." Courtney waved him off.

"I'll just wait here, then."

"Have fun." Isabella's voice was muffled from her face being pressed against the towel.

"Okay." Canyon plopped down on the sand.

"Seriously?" Courtney threw him a sideways glance.

"Yeah. I have nothing better to do." He leaned back and rested his head against his palms. The hot sand burned against the back of his hands, but he didn't move them.

"Come on, Bella." Courtney's tone was whiny. "Just talk to him."

"Nope," came Isabella's muffled reply.

"It's fine." Canyon kicked one ankle over the other. "I've got all the time in the world."

Both of Isabella's friends urged her to talk to him. She finally relented, shooting him a death glare. "You have two minutes."

"Sure thing." He jumped to his feet and dusted sand from his clothes.

"Talk." Isabella stared at him expectantly.

"Not here."

She threw her hands in the air. "Fine."

Canyon strode over to an area shaded by trees and waited for her to catch up.

"What do you want?"

He stuck his hands in his pants' pockets and held her gaze. "For you to stop meddling. Stop discouraging Maggie from spending time with me."

She narrowed her eyes. "I'll do no such thing."

"Why not?"

"Because she's my friend, and I don't want to see her getting hurt."

"And why do you assume I'll hurt her?"

"You really have to ask?"

Canyon leaned forward. "Yeah, actually I do."

"Because you're a womanizer, that's why. You go from one woman to the next without stopping to take a breath between. Maggie deserves better. She's not the flavor of the hour."

"What makes you think you know me so well?"

Isabella's nostrils flared. "I've seen you in action, stupid!"

He gave her a double-take. "Excuse me?"

"You don't remember when I was vacationing on your cruise line?"

Canyon wracked his thoughts but couldn't recall having seen her at work at any point.

"You are so dense." She huffed. "I saw you making out with five different people—on a three-day cruise! Others have seen the same thing."

His stomach tightened. There was no way he could deny her accusations. She was probably right.

"See? You can't even defend yourself. I'm going back to my friends now."

Canyon stepped closer to her. "Not yet, you're not. I can't deny what you saw, but what I can assure you is that I'm different now. All of that is in the past."

She snorted. "Once a pig, always a pig."

Anger surged through him, but he took a deep breath and counted to twenty in his mind. "The only person I have eyes for is Maggie. I've already turned down opportunities to have stupid flings since I got here. I've given up my old lifestyle. Don't you think I'd still be working on the cruise boats if that's what I wanted?"

Isabella pursed her lips. "With all the tourists coming and going, you have plenty of new people to pick from."

"What about the rest of the year?"

She shrugged. "I'm sure you're creative."

He clenched his jaw. "Look, I care about Maggie. I'm in

love with her. I'd do anything for her, and that includes treating her like the treasure she is. I would appreciate if you'd stop getting in the way of that."

Isabella stared at him but didn't say anything. Was he finally getting through to her?

"Tell me this." He stepped even closer. "Have you seen me with any other woman since I've been back?"

She didn't respond.

"Have you seen me with anyone other than Maggie? We've crossed paths countless times. Was I with anyone else even once?"

"No. Okay?"

"Isn't that proof that I've changed? According to your math, I should've been with, what, fifteen people by now? Yet the only person I can think about is Maggie. Not one other woman has even caught my attention."

Isabella took a deep breath. "You really want me to stop discouraging her from seeing you?"

"Yes!"

She stared him down. "On one condition."

"What is it?"

"And if you break it, all bets are off."

"What's your condition?" Canyon demanded.

"If you so much as hurt her in the slightest, you walk away. For good."

"I wouldn't ever do anything to hurt her!"

"Then we won't have any problems. If I see you even looking at another woman, all bets are off. If I hear rumors of you with another woman, all bets are off. You treat her like a princess, and I won't say a thing about you to her."

"It's a deal." He held out a hand to shake on it.

"Seriously?"

"Shake on it. I'm a man of my word."

"You'd better be." Isabella shook his hand, eyeing him like

he was a viper. At least she'd agreed to stop getting in between him and Maggie. She spun around and marched back to her towel, stopping only to glance back for a moment. "One wrong move, and you walk away!"

"That's the deal!"

CHAPTER 23

M aggie glanced at Canyon's text again to make sure she had the right meeting spot. They were going to meet in a dark alley between two buildings.

The whole thing was rather ridiculous, but she wasn't going to let her aunt stop her from seeing Canyon. Once Maggie had enough money to find a place to rent, she could date him openly.

The alley was only a couple blocks away. She glanced up and down the street to make sure nobody was paying her any attention. They weren't.

Her phone rang. Excited to talk to Canyon, she went to answer it. But it was Dan again.

That was the reminder she needed to block his number. Maggie stopped and waited for the ringing to stop. Then she blocked him. She felt triumphant.

Now she wouldn't have to think about him again. He was officially out of her life for good.

She practically skipped toward the alleyway. Before she arrived, Canyon's car pulled up.

He rolled down the passenger window. "Get in the back-seat and hide under the blanket I put there."

"For real?"

"Yeah. Hurry up!"

She laughed at the absurdity of it but climbed into the back.

"Under the blanket so nobody sees you. I can think of more than a dozen people who would gladly tell Lucille about seeing us together."

Maggie reclined over the length of the seat, then pulled the queen-size quilt over her. "How long do I have to stay this way?"

"At least until we're out of Indigo Bay. You okay back there? Can you buckle up?"

"I can try." She fought with the middle seat belt, managing to maneuver it diagonally across her.

It clicked into place.

She waited as the car bumped along. "How much longer?"

"Not much. So, how was your day?"

Maggie pulled the blanket out an inch for air. "I got a job working for Violet Montgomery's cousin."

"Nice. Think that'll be enough to move out?"

"It'll be a start. I'm not sure it'll last more than a week, but at least it's something. I can look for another job on my breaks."

"I can chip in," Canyon offered.

"No, you have your own rent to pay for."

"Still, you have to move out because of me. I feel like I should do something to help."

"Don't worry about it. I should've gotten my own place long ago. Bumming off my aunt at my age is ludicrous."

He laughed. "I'm living at my mom's, and I'm a year older than you."

"You're at least paying rent, and besides, you just got to town. I've been here for a year. I have no excuse."

"Oh, you're fine."

She slid a little as the car took a sharp turn.

"You can sit up now. We're safely outside town."

Maggie sat up and gasped in the fresh air. "Next time, you're in the backseat."

"As you wish."

"Princess Bride?"

"Huh?" He glanced at her through the rear-view mirror.

"You just quoted the movie. We used to watch that, remember?"

Canyon grinned. "I forgot all about that. Those were good times."

She smiled, too. "They sure were."

They reminisced for a while until Canyon finally pulled into the parking lot in front of a tiny building.

"What's this?"

"You'll see." He winked at her through the mirror. After parking, he held open the back door for her, then ran his fingers through her hair. "Just trying to fix it after the blanket. I like the messy look, though."

Her cheeks warmed as she glanced at her reflection in the window. "Really?"

"Really." Canyon kissed her cheek, then threaded his fingers through hers.

Maggie squeezed his hand and studied the building. It was made of stone, had vines growing up the side, and there were several cracks in the blocks. "You won't tell me what this place is?"

"I said you'll see." He tucked some of her hair behind her ear, then led her to the door. A mixture of greasy hamburgers, fries, and fresh ice cream cones filled the air.

Inside, all the employees behind the counter wore black

and white outfits reminiscent of the nineteen-fifties. "Jail-house Rock" played from a juke box off to the side.

Canyon turned to her. "You'll never have a better burger than at this place. Trust me. I've had burgers all over the world."

They placed their orders and then sat in a booth near the back, surrounded by posters of *Happy Days* and *I Love Lucy*.

"Do you come here often?"

Canyon placed his arm around her. "This was my brother's and my favorite restaurant. We'd beg our parents to bring us here all the time."

"I can see why. This place is great."

"Wait until you try the food."

The cashier called out Canyon's name.

He kissed Maggie's temple. "Be right back." A minute later, he came back, balancing a full tray of burgers, fries, and shakes. "Dig in."

She unwrapped the foil and bit into the messy burger with lettuce falling out. It practically melted into her mouth.

Canyon wiped his mouth. "Good, huh?"

Maggie swallowed. "How have I never been here before?"

He snickered. "I have a hard time picturing Lucille coming here."

She laughed. "That's true."

They finished eating, then Canyon put his arm around her. "There's a waterfall just a short hike from here."

"Really? That sounds romantic." She snuggled closer to him.

"I haven't been there since I was a kid, so that was the furthest thing from my mind back then. But going with you would be extremely romantic."

They gathered the wrappers and tossed them in the garbage before heading outside. Canyon slid his fingers through hers, and they headed toward the trees on the other side of the building. They followed a well-worn path until they came to a rock wall with water gushing down into a bubbling pool.

Maggie gasped. "It's so beautiful."

"It pales in comparison to you." Canyon cupped her chin in both his palms, then brushed his lips across hers.

Her heart raced and breath caught. There was nothing that she loved more than this. Being so close to Canyon that she could smell his rugged scent. It made the sneaking around worth risking her aunt's wrath until she found a place to live.

She'd continue sneaking around for the rest of her life for moments like this if she had to.

CHAPTER 24

The following week went by in a blur of working on the house and sneaking dates with Maggie in the evenings and all day on the weekend.

Canyon loved every moment with her, and Isabella kept her word, feigning friendship with him on the rare occasion he ran into the two of them together at Sweet Caroline's or the beach.

He could hardly believe how well everything was going. Every day their relationship grew better. His breath hitched each time Maggie looked at him. It was clear she felt the same way about him that he felt about her—and that still shocked him.

Never once had he imagined it was possible. Now that it was actually happening, he half-expected to wake up on the boat and find it all to be a dream. But it kept up, day after day, and was now closing in on two weeks.

His phone buzzed with a text, pulling him from his thoughts. It was Maggie, asking about their secret date of the day. They texted back and forth for a few minutes, securing the details.

After dinners at home separately to save money, they would meet at a secluded part of the beach, hidden nicely by trees and some other plant life. It had started to become their place, though they'd been careful not to go there two days in a row, but it was where they went more often than not.

The day dragged on until he was finally heading over to the beach. He gave some friendly hellos to people he passed along the way and finally made it to their spot.

Maggie already sat there, leaning against a tree and staring at the water. As usual, she took his breath away. She was actually there to see him. Again.

Canyon glanced around to make sure nobody was looking his way, then he casually strolled over, though he wanted to sprint.

She turned toward him and gave him her gorgeous smile. He threw his arms around her and spun her in a circle.

Maggie laughed then gave him a quick kiss. "Was it just me, or did today drag on and on?"

"It totally dragged." He kissed her back and set her down. "But now everything is right in the world again."

"Almost." She glanced over at the full beach.

"Sure, it'd be better if we could actually date openly. At least we can be together. It beats not seeing you."

Her eyes lit up. "That's true. I—" Maggie's smile faded and she stared at something behind him.

Canyon spun around but didn't see anything out of the ordinary. "What's wrong?"

"I… I can't believe he's here."

"Who?"

She stumbled back a few steps but didn't answer.

Canyon studied the crowd and noticed one guy heading their way. He was blond and unnaturally tan with extra-white teeth. Not only that, but he wore long khakis and a dress shirt—hardly beachwear. As the guy got closer,

Canyon noticed he had beady little eyes and a smug expression.

Canyon turned back to Maggie, her face was pale. "Who's that?"

She swallowed. "It's Dan."

"Dan?" Somehow that made sense. Maybe because everything about him shouted that he was a slimeball. "As in your ex-fiancé?"

Maggie nodded, still looking past Canyon.

"What on earth is he doing here?" Canyon's stomach twisted in knots so tight he wasn't sure they'd ever unravel.

She just shook her head.

"Did you know he was coming?" He realized that was a dumb question as soon as it escaped his lips. She looked like she was seeing a ghost.

"No." Maggie stumbled back again.

"You don't know why he's here?"

"I have no idea."

Dan sauntered over, glared at Canyon, then rested his gaze on Maggie. "I've been trying to call you."

She swallowed. "I blocked your number."

"Why would you do that?"

Canyon put his arm around Maggie. "Because she doesn't want to talk to you. Time to leave."

Dan glared at him. "Who are you?"

"Someone who will protect Maggie. That's all you need to know."

"She doesn't need protection from me."

"Then why did she block your number?" Canyon countered.

Dan's brows came together. "Would you give us some privacy? I need to talk to her."

Canyon tightened his hold around Maggie's shoulders. "Doesn't seem like she wants to talk to you."

The other man shook his head and turned back to Maggie. "We need to talk."

"We have nothing to talk about. How did you find me here, anyway?"

"I followed you from your aunt's house."

"How dare you!" Maggie stiffened against Canyon.

Canyon stood taller.

Dan glanced back and forth between Maggie and Canyon, then glowered. "Guess I'll have to tell you with him here." He said *him* like Canyon was toxic waste.

Maggie stepped forward, standing tall. "We have nothing to talk about."

"You need to hear this, Maggie."

She shook her head. "After the way you treated me, no. I don't owe you anything."

Dan's expression softened. "No, but I do. You need to hear what I have to say."

"What?"

He stepped closer to Maggie.

Canyon clenched his fists, ready to pummel him if need be.

Dan held Maggie's gaze for a moment before speaking. "The doctor's office called me. There was a mistake with the test. They are wrong."

"Wh-what do you mean?"

"You can have kids, Magnolia. I don't know all the details, but your results were switched with someone else's. I didn't find out more because I wanted to tell you the news as soon as I could. Since you wouldn't talk to me over the phone, I had to come here personally."

Canyon stepped forward. "Why wouldn't the doctor's office call *her*? Seems odd they'd give you the news. Privacy laws and all that legal stuff, you know."

Dan flicked him an annoyed glance. "Small-town doctor. They'll tell just about anything to her *fiancé*."

"Ex," Canyon corrected.

"Whatever." Dan turned back to Maggie. "We can get married, after all. Isn't this great news? That house you fell in love with is still for sale, but the housing market is improving in that area, so we'll have to act quickly."

Canyon stared at Dan. He couldn't be serious? Did he really expect Maggie would run back to him?

Maggie stood, shaking.

"Are you okay?" Canyon whispered and pulled her closer.

CHAPTER 25

Maggie could barely remain standing as the news sunk in. She could actually have kids! The medical report had been a mistake. Someone else's bad news.

The doctor had told her that there was irreparable damage to her fallopian tubes. But now it wasn't true. Her tubes were normal!

She struggled to breathe normally, to take in deep breaths. The whole world seemed to have disappeared around her since Dan said she could have kids. She hadn't heard another word he'd said after that.

Her dreams of having a family could really happen. If things kept going so well with Canyon and they got married —it could be a possibility now!—she could give him children of his own.

She wasn't defective, like Dan had made her feel when the test results had originally come in.

Was he telling the truth, or was this some cruel game? He'd shown a whole new side of himself after they found out she couldn't have kids. Or maybe it wasn't new, but he'd been hiding it.

Both Dan and Canyon were speaking, but their words sounded far away. Muffled. Like they were speaking through water.

Maggie gasped for air, starting to feel lightheaded.

She needed to get away. By herself. Think and let the news settle. Then once she could string together a coherent sentence or two, she needed to speak with the doctor herself.

Without a word, Maggie burst into a run. She stumbled in the sand but didn't let that slow her. She nearly crashed into a few people but barely noticed.

Once at the street, she kept going. Everything passed by in a blur. Tears stung her eyes. Her muscles burned and her heart felt like it would give out.

Everything seemed to press in toward her, wanting to crush her. Maggie just kept running until she made it past the main part of town and came to some abandoned buildings and a big open field. She wasn't even sure she was still in Indigo Bay anymore.

Exhausted, she leaned against a dilapidated wall and gasped for air. It felt a lot better to focus on that than anything else.

Did she dare hope Dan's news was true? It could just be another ploy. A way to control and manipulate her.

Maggie closed her eyes and waited for the world to stop spinning. She slid down the wall until she was sitting and rested her head against her knees.

What if Dan was telling the truth? If he was, that meant her fling—relationship?—with Canyon could potentially turn into something more. She wanted that like she'd wanted nothing else before, but she hadn't let herself believe it could truly happen. Not a *real* future. An actual family.

What was she going to do?

Maggie reached into her pocket for the phone but shook too much to be able to grab it. She needed to talk to the doctor, but she couldn't even calm down enough to grab her phone.

Tears blurred her vision, then they spilled to her face. She gasped for air before giving into the sobs.

For some reason, she cried harder now than she had when she'd first received the bad news. The tears wouldn't stop.

As she cried, the sky changed colors until it finally grew dark and glimmered with twinkling stars. Maggie stared at them, at last free of the tears.

She located the Big Dipper and studied it. Would she be able to teach her future children how to find it? Would she be able to teach them all the things she'd dreamed about for so long, until the day the nurse called with the news?

Her mind wandered, old dusty dreams coming back to life.

Did she dare hope?

It was too late to call the office now. She'd have to wait until the morning to find out if Dan was telling the truth. But why else would he come all the way to Indigo Bay from Georgia? He wouldn't do that for a trick, would he?

Maybe, but that seemed too vicious, even for him.

He had to be telling the truth. But why? What else had he said?

She strained to remember, but everything after telling her that she could have kids was a blur. Like trying to remember a dream that was fading like sand from an hourglass.

What was so important about the news that he'd left his fiancée and come to tell her about this personally? He'd had to have driven for hours—when he could've called Aunt Lucille's house and just told her.

Exhaustion swept over her, making her muscles feel like rubber. She drew in a deep breath and rested her head against the wall.

What she needed was to climb into bed and sleep. Let her mind process everything through dreams.

Then she could wake in the morning, call the office, and find out if what Dan said was really true.

If only she could get her legs to cooperate.

CHAPTER 26

Canyon turned to Dan, fuming. They'd searched all over Indigo Bay and hadn't been able to find Maggie. "Great work!"

"Hey, I told you I didn't expect her to run off."

"Right, because her blocking your number didn't clue you in on the fact that she wants nothing to do with you."

Dan's nostrils flared. "Now that she knows she can have kids, that changes everything. We can get married now."

"You're unbelievable!"

"What?" Dan actually sounded clueless.

"Aren't you engaged to someone else?"

He shook his head. "Not anymore. Her family lost their fortune."

"So you dumped her?"

"Of course."

Maggie had sure dodged a bullet not marrying this piece of work.

Canyon squinted and looked up and down the beach for what had to be the hundredth time. "Is anyone good enough for you?"

"Maggie is, now that she can give me boys to carry on my legacy."

"If the results were fake, she could've done that the whole time, couldn't she?"

"Yeah, but I didn't know that. You honestly don't have a clue where she would've went?"

It took all of Canyon's effort not to break Dan's nose. "If I knew, do you think we'd still be looking?"

"Maybe we should report her missing."

"Missing?" Canyon exclaimed. "She's avoiding *you*."

Dan's expression twisted. "I didn't see her taking you with her. Seems she's avoiding both of us."

"You know what? We'd be better off searching separately. Cover more ground and all that."

Dan's scowl faded. "You might be onto something. Maybe you should call the police."

"Or maybe you should, since this is all your fault. Better yet, tell Lucille. She could probably round up a search party faster than the cops with her connections."

"You think so?"

Canyon threw his arms into the air. "Do you know Maggie's family at all?"

"More than you."

Canyon waved him off, then marched down the street toward his home. He'd already looked there, hoping Maggie had gone there. She hadn't, but that had been over an hour earlier.

She still wasn't there. His heart sank past his stomach and shattered on the ground.

Where was she?

She hadn't posted any updates on her social media profiles. His calls kept going to voicemail.

Maybe the next attempt would be the exception.

Canyon pulled out his phone and called Maggie again.

It rang and rang…

Then voicemail.

He threw his head back in frustration, then left another message pleading with her to return the call. But if she was ignoring his other messages, this one wouldn't make a difference.

After hanging up, he sent her a quick text: *Can you just let me know you're okay?*

Canyon waited a minute, hoping against hope. Then he bolted down the street and stopped everyone he came across, asking if they'd seen her.

Nobody had.

Isabella was climbing into her car a block and a half away.

Canyon sprinted toward her, calling out her name.

She glanced up and stepped away from her car.

He reached her, out of breath.

"What's going on?"

"H… have you… seen Maggie?"

"Don't tell me you got her in trouble!" She held up a fist and shook it in his face.

"No! It was Dan!"

"Dan? Her ex-fiancé?"

"The one and only. He showed up, upset her, then she bolted. That was before the sun went down."

Isabella's mouth dropped. "What?"

"Do you know where she might've gone? I've looked everywhere I can think of at least twice."

"Have you tried calling her?"

"What do you think?" Canyon snapped.

"Let me try. Maybe she needs a friend right now."

"I'm going to keep looking. Call me if you hear from her."

"I don't have your number."

"Right." They exchanged numbers, then he ran down the road continuing to ask everyone in sight if they'd seen her.

He passed Sweet Caroline's. Perhaps if someone had seen Maggie, they had told Caroline.

Canyon rushed in and pushed himself next to the person at the register. That earned him a dirty look.

"Everything okay, Canyon?" Caroline asked.

"No. Have you seen Maggie? Or heard anything about her?"

Caroline froze. "What happened?"

"It would take too long to explain. If you hear anything, please let me know!"

"Certainly. And the same goes for you. I want to hear the moment you learn anything."

Canyon nodded, hoping he'd remember given his current state of mind. He raced outside and headed for Lucille's neighborhood.

Blue and red lights bounced off the large houses, though they were set off from the road.

The police were already there. That could be good news or bad, depending on what Dan had told them. He'd have certainly painted Canyon in the worst possible way, and Lucille would've gladly gone along with it.

He spun around to go the other way.

"Canyon!"

His entire body tensed. Reluctantly, he turned around.

Officer Moore stood in front of Lucille's house, a flashlight aimed at Canyon.

He was tempted to run, but that would only make him look guilty. And he'd done nothing wrong. He took a deep breath. "Officer Moore."

"Where have you been, son?"

Canyon wanted to say he wasn't Moore's son. Instead, he made a point to relax his stance. "Out trying to find Maggie, sir."

"You were the last one to see her?"

"Dan, her ex, and I were. After he showed up unannounced and gave her upsetting news."

"Why don't you come with me?" Officer Moore nodded toward Lucille's house.

Great.

"Sure thing. Anything to help find Maggie." Canyon was impressed with himself for keeping his tone so light.

They walked down the walkway. The heavily-flowered air tickled his nose. He'd never before seen so many roses or bluestars in one place. Canyon wouldn't know what bluestars were, but Lucille made a point to make sure everyone in town knew about her prize flowers.

Inside the enormous home, Lucille and Dan sat on a large sofa, speaking with another policeman.

"Canyon's here," Moore announced.

Lucille jumped up, her eyes wild and red. "What have you done to my Maggie?"

"Nothing." He glared at Dan. "You should be asking him."

"Why?" Lucille gave Canyon a sideways glance.

"Because if he hadn't showed up, Maggie wouldn't have run off."

Lucille tilted her head. "And how would you know that?"

Canyon bit his tongue to give him a moment to think before saying what he wanted to—Lucille was bound to slap him if he did speak his thoughts. "We ran into each other at the beach when he showed up."

Dan snorted. "Ran into each other. Right. You two looked pretty cozy when I saw you."

"We *did* run into each other there—you'd know that since you admitted to following her there!"

His mouth dropped. "It's your word against mine."

"Until Maggie shows up to tell you otherwise."

They stared each other down.

Officer Moore stepped in between them. "Perhaps we should question you two separately."

"Question me?" Canyon exclaimed. "Maggie ran off! Nobody has seen her—we need to get out there and find her! She's missing."

Dan glowered at him. "You told me she wasn't missing."

"That was before I had a chance to ask half the town if they'd seen her."

"You're a real peach."

Canyon held back an eye roll. "You're one to talk."

"Come on." Officer Moore gestured toward another room. "Let's talk in here."

Canyon glared at Dan. If only looks could kill…

CHAPTER 27

Maggie opened her eyes. She was lying on the ground, staring at an open field with overgrown grass and empty bottles strewn across one side. Based on the sun being low in east, it was morning.

She sat up, gasping for air. It took a moment to figure out how she'd gotten there.

Then everything from the night before flooded her mind. Her interrupted date with Canyon. Dan giving her the news that had shocked her to the core.

She could have kids. A family. Marriage.

After she'd written it all off as impossible and accepted the harsh reality.

She needed to find out if Dan was telling the truth. Did she still have the doctor's office in her phone?

Maggie went to her contact list and found the number.

Her heart skipped a beat. Maybe two.

She took a deep breath and held it before pressing call.

It rang. She almost hung up. She almost *threw* up.

"Dr. Stanton's office. Please hold."

"O-okay." Instrumental music played. She was already on hold.

Maggie pushed herself to her feet and dusted dirt, sand, and pebbles from her clothes.

"Thanks for holding. How may I help you?"

Maggie cleared her throat. "My name's Magnolia Kendrick and your office told my ex-fiancé that a test result from a couple years ago was wrong. I'm calling to find out about that."

"Oh, right. Magnolia. Yes, we received a call from the hospital about that. Your file was swapped with another patient's. There was a problem with one of their employees, but I'm not at liberty to go into the details about that."

Yet they were okay with telling her ex-fiancé about the mixup over the phone?

The woman continued, "They hospital has generously offered to redo the test for you free of charge if you would feel better about it."

She swallowed. "To be clear, all it was was a mixup of the results? My actual result was clear?"

"I'm not at liberty to go into details because of privacy laws. But I can tell you the files were mixed up. Would you like to schedule that appointment to have the scan done again?"

"Were my results normal? Can you tell me that much?"

She spoke in a quieter tone. "Yes, they were."

Maggie breathed a sigh of relief. "Can I think about rescheduling the test? I'm out of state right now."

"Sure thing, darlin'. Just give us a call, and we'll get it all set up for you."

Maggie thanked her and ended the call. It was true. She could have kids.

One call, and the trajectory of her life had changed.

Beads of sweat broke out on her forehead. She needed to

get back home—to Aunt Lucille's—and get freshened up and take an ibuprofen. Sleeping on the ground hadn't been the best idea.

Maggie twisted her neck and it popped loudly, then she headed in the direction she was pretty sure she'd come from. The details of the previous night were blurry after seeing Dan.

She seemed to walk forever through empty fields and alleys between old buildings. It had been twenty minutes, and she still hadn't reached Indigo Bay.

How far had she run before finally stopping?

Finally, about five minutes later she came to an area she recognized. It would still be another fifteen minutes or so to Aunt Lucille's house, depending on how quickly she could get could her feet to move. Her legs ached something fierce, and each step was harder than the last. It didn't help that sun was growing hotter and shade was hard to come by on the side of the road she was on.

After what felt like forever, the house finally came into view. Maggie nearly collapsed with relief right where she stood. But she pressed on, and finally made it to the front door.

She fumbled with her keys, and the door opened before she actually slid the key into the hole.

"Maggie!" Aunt Lucille stood in front of her in yesterday's dress with messy hair and smeared makeup. She pulled Maggie in and closed the door. "Where have you been?"

Dan appeared behind her.

Maggie's heart sank. "What's he doing here?"

Auntie's face reddened. "You don't get to ask the questions. Where were you?"

Maggie glared at Dan. "I needed some space."

"Didn't you think to call anyone? Everyone has been

looking for you! We've all called you, not that it did any good."

"I needed space after *he* showed up. Why is he here?"

"I've invited him to stay in one of the guest rooms as long as he needs to. Enough about him. Why didn't you at least let anyone know you were safe?"

Maggie frowned. "You're right. I should have, but I was too upset to think. I'm sorry you were worried, Auntie."

Aunt Lucille opened her mouth, but then closed it and pulled Maggie into a hug. "Don't do that ever again. I've never been so worried in all my life."

Maggie nodded and wrapped her arms around her aunt. Once they parted, Maggie made eye contact. "Can you please send Dan on his way?"

"He was as worried as I was."

"All of this was his fault!"

Aunt Lucille put her hand on Maggie's shoulder. "Let's all get showered, then we can talk over breakfast."

"But—"

"No arguments. We all need to freshen up."

Maggie narrowed her eyes as she passed Dan.

He reached out for her. "Maggie—"

"No!" She ran up the stairs and locked herself in her room, never more relieved to have her own bathroom. She would avoid Dan as long as she could, until her aunt insisted she come down for food.

Her stomach rumbled at the thought.

It would have to wait. Maggie was going to take the longest, hottest shower in the history of the world before she even thought about eating since Dan was staying in the same house.

What made her aunt think that was a good idea? Was she so desperate to set Maggie up with someone other than

Canyon, that her next effort was the one person who had hurt Maggie more than anyone else ever had?

Yes, they definitely needed to have a talk—a long one where Maggie explained everything, including how Dan had treated her after finding out about the mistaken medical report. Surely, that would convince Aunt Lucille to send him back to Georgia.

CHAPTER 28

C anyon stopped hammering the moment his phone buzzed in his pocket. It had to be news on Maggie.

Isabella was calling.

"Did you find her?" Canyon answered.

"Lucille just called and said she's home. Looks like a wreck, but is otherwise fine."

He breathed a sigh of relief and leaned against the newly refinished kitchen counter. "Where was she?"

"Lucille doesn't know, and I haven't actually talked to Maggie myself. Just wanted to let you know."

"Thank you, Isabella."

"Sure. Talk to you later." The call ended.

Harry walked into the room and wiped sweat from his brow. "Everything okay in here?"

"Maggie's back. Can I take my break early and go see her for myself? Either that, or I'll work late. Or this weekend. I just have to go and see her now."

The older man gave him a sympathetic glance. "Scram."

"Thank you!" Canyon stuffed his phone back into his

pants' pocket and bolted out of the house and into his car. He made record time getting to Lucille's.

He brushed dust from his clothes and ran his fingers through his hair before walking up the walkway, trying not to think about the previous night with the cops. The only thing that mattered was that Maggie was okay.

Canyon knocked loudly, not wanting to ring the doorbell so early.

The door opened a crack. Dan appeared.

Dan. In the same home Maggie was staying in.

Canyon clenched his jaw as the two men stared each other down.

"Maggie's home and safe." Dan narrowed his eyes. "You can leave now."

"I want to see her."

He shook his head. "She's in the shower. I'll tell her you stopped by."

"Right. Let me in."

"No. Lucille doesn't want you in her house. Go away."

"You can't keep me from seeing Maggie."

Dan inched the door closer to the frame. "No, but she can. We're working through things now that she's confirmed the truth of the test results."

"You're lying."

"Actually, I'm not. We're going to discuss wedding plans over breakfast. Leave before we have to file a restraining order. Buh-bye." Dan slammed the door shut. Locks clicked into place.

Canyon stared at the door as anger pulsated through him.

"Go away!" Dan's muffled voice came from the other side.

"You might be able to keep me away from Lucille's house, but you can't keep me from Maggie!"

"I'm calling Officer Moore right now."

Canyon spun around and stormed back to his car. There

was no way Maggie was actually planning on getting back together with that man. Not after everything she'd told Canyon about him.

No. If Dan was telling the truth, he'd have let Canyon in to hear it from Maggie. The fact that he wouldn't even let Canyon see inside meant that he was lying through his teeth.

He sent Maggie a quick text before heading back to work. Driving nails into the wall would be the perfect way to get his frustration out.

"Is she okay?" Harry asked when Canyon returned.

Canyon only nodded before heading back to the kitchen and picking up his hammer.

The hours flew by, and before he knew it, Harry announced that it was time for lunch. Though Canyon's stomach rumbled, he didn't feel hungry. The only thing he wanted was to talk with Maggie.

Once in his car again, he called Maggie but it went straight to voicemail. He hit the steering wheel.

What was going on? Had Dan hidden her phone from her? Turned it off? Or was Maggie sleeping the day away?

Canyon just wanted answers, but he couldn't get them at Lucille's house. He headed for home, not wanting to see anyone, and forced himself to eat, knowing he needed the fuel to get through the rest of the day.

No calls or texts from Maggie.

It was as though she was being held prisoner. Or was it him? Lucille and Dan were keeping her from him like he was some kind of criminal. They were making him pay for having feelings for Maggie.

He sent her a quick text offering to meet her anywhere, anytime.

For all he knew, Dan or Lucille were screening her calls and texts.

That was the only thing that made any sense. Why else wouldn't Maggie contact him?

Canyon cleaned his dishes, then paced the house, his mind racing. He had to do something, but what?

The only thing he could think of was to return to their spot on the beach after work and wait. All on the off chance that she might return there since it was the one place they'd secretly met more times than any other place.

CHAPTER 29

Maggie's stomach growled. She'd barely had two bites of food before leaving the table at breakfast. It had been obvious that Dan had won over Aunt Lucille, and neither of them wanted to hear a single thing she had to say.

It made sense. Dan was a smooth talker. He knew how to say whatever people wanted to hear and make them believe he meant every word. That was why Maggie's eyes hadn't been opened to his true nature until the mixed-up test result came in.

In a way, the bad news had been the best news. It had freed her from him, though it had crushed her at the time. Losing the ability to bear children was hard enough without losing her fiancé, too.

She almost wanted to find the employee who had messed up the test results and kiss him.

Maggie stared at her door, wanting to leave the room but not wanting to run into either Dan or her aunt.

Dan had already let her know that he was in his room, waiting for her to emerge.

Her stomach twisted at the thought. It was enough to

leave her considering the window as her only escape, but she was two stories up and there was nothing underneath. If she was one room over, she'd be able to use one of the sprawling decks.

More than anything, she wanted to talk to Canyon but it was the middle of his work day. Maybe she should send him a quick text. That way he would at least know she was thinking of him.

She went over to the desk, where she'd set her phone after arriving.

It wasn't there.

Maggie had locked the door when she'd come in—she was sure of it. She'd come inside, twisted the lock, and put the phone down on the desk before pulling off the dirty clothes.

Yet the phone was gone. Both Lucille and Dan had been waiting for her when she stepped into the hallway after her shower, and neither had left her side until she'd bolted from the dining room table.

That could only mean that one of them had unlocked her bedroom door and taken the phone while she was in the shower.

Had they gotten into any of her other things? She looked around, her pulse racing, but didn't notice anything out of place.

Was that Dan's scheme to get her out of the bedroom? Or was he doing something else with it? She had a passcode set, so he couldn't do anything other than make an emergency call.

Maggie flung open the door and only took a few steps before Dan stepped in front of her.

"How are you feeling, Magnolia?"

"Where's my phone?" she demanded.

"It's charging downstairs."

She stepped around him and raced down the stairs.

"Where are you going? We still need to talk."

Maggie ignored him and glanced around for her phone, not seeing it. Maybe it was in the kitchen.

It wasn't.

Dan caught up to her. "Why do you keep avoiding me?"

She spun around and glared at him. "And why can't you take a clue? We're *through*. You're the one who ended things, remember?"

"But now we can be together again. Everything's good."

"You didn't want me when you thought I couldn't have kids! That was all it took for you to throw me away like a bag of trash. You don't get a second chance after that. Where's my phone?"

Aunt Lucille walked into the room. "Is that true?"

Dan's face paled.

Anger pulsated through Maggie. Now that she finally had her aunt's attention, she filled her in on everything Dan had done and said after finding out she couldn't have kids.

Aunt Lucille's face turned redder than it had been when Maggie arrived earlier. She narrowed her eyes and stepped closer to Dan. "Get out of my house now, and never return!"

"But I—"

"Now!"

Dan turned around and scrambled up the stairs.

"Where did you put my phone?" Maggie called.

He didn't respond.

Aunt Lucille pulled Maggie into a second embrace. "Why didn't you tell me any of that? You really thought you were barren all this time?"

Maggie nodded. "It was too painful to talk about, especially after the way Dan broke up with me."

"You poor thing. If I'd had any idea, I wouldn't have kept trying to set you up with all the respectable men in town."

"I know you just wanted me to be happy. I didn't have the heart to tell you nobody would want me."

Lucille stepped back but kept her hands on Maggie's shoulders. "Not want you? Are you mad, child? Any man would be *lucky* to have you for a wife, barren or not."

Maggie looked away, embarrassed.

"I'm sorry for interfering. Is there anything I can do to make it up to you?"

She turned to Aunt Lucille. "There is one thing."

"What, dear?"

"Give Canyon a chance."

Auntie's expression tightened. "Do you know how he treats women?"

Maggie stood taller. "Canyon treats *me* with nothing but respect. He's changed his ways and regrets his past actions. And more importantly, he cares about me whether I can have kids or not."

Aunt Lucille took a deep breath. "I'll give him a chance for your sake."

"Thank you, Auntie."

Dan raced down the stairs, a single bag over his shoulder, and hurried to the front door without looking at either of them.

"Where's my phone?" Maggie demanded again.

He didn't respond, other than slamming the door on his way out.

Maggie threw her arms into the air and turned back to her aunt. "Do you know where it is?"

"I saw a phone charging in Dan's room."

Maggie rushed up the stairs, skipping every other step, and stopped in the room Dan had been staying in. Sure enough, her phone sat on the dresser, charging.

She unlocked it with the passcode and went to her texting conversation with Canyon.

It wasn't there.

Maggie went to her contacts. His name and number were also missing. She checked the call log. Nothing from Canyon.

Dan had cleared everything from Canyon from her phone. Not only that, but he'd unblocked his number and left her several text messages, declaring his love for her.

She shook, feeling violated.

Had he figured out her code or found another way into the phone?

Maggie deleted his texts and re-blocked his number.

Now to find Canyon since she couldn't call or text him.

She raced outside to her car, calling a quick goodbye to her aunt on the way out.

When she got to the little house, Canyon's car wasn't outside. Maybe he'd walked to work that day.

Maggie ran inside and found Harry in the kitchen. "Where's Canyon?"

"It's good to see you, Maggie. I'm not sure where he is. He hasn't returned from lunch. Didn't say anything about a long lunch."

Maggie frowned. Where would he have gone?

CHAPTER 30

C anyon stared at the water lapping up to the shore. As much as pounding nails had sounded like a good stress reliever, he hadn't been able to bring himself to go back to work.

Not after the text she'd sent him.

Though it was a bright and beautiful day, it felt like dark clouds were descending on him. Maggie had been back at Lucille's since the morning, and that was all the time it had taken her to change her mind about everything.

Not that he could blame her, really. Dan could give Maggie so much that he couldn't with his fancy job and big house. From what Canyon knew about him, his family had even more money than Lucille's.

Maggie could live in the lap of luxury, like she was used to. All Canyon could offer her was love. He couldn't afford the nice clothes or expensive jewelry Maggie always wore.

If he was being honest with himself, he'd been pretty dumb to think they could make things work. She was used to one way of life, and he lived another.

And maybe with the new medical report, Dan would treat

143

her well. That was all he could ask—that she would be happy. If Dan would do that much, Canyon could live with them being together.

He took a deep breath, grabbed some stones, then strolled to the water's edge. After studying the surface, he threw the first one. It skipped four times before sinking.

The next one also skipped four times. Why could he never get one to go five?

"Do you have an extra rock?"

Canyon's heart broke at the sound of Maggie's voice. He turned around and forced a smile as he held out the remaining stones. "Sure."

She smiled sweetly and took one.

It was all he could do to hold himself together. He nodded and turned back to the water. It hurt too much to look at her when she'd agreed to give her heart to another.

Maggie flung the stone out into the bay.

It bounced five times.

He dropped the rest of them.

She turned to him, but he couldn't do the same.

"Are you okay?" she asked.

"Sure."

A beat of silence rested between them.

"I'm sorry I didn't call you."

Canyon shrugged. "It's fine."

More silence.

"Why won't you look at me? I thought you'd be happy to see me. Or are you mad?"

He cleared his throat. "I could never be mad at you, Maggie."

"Then look at me."

Canyon turned, but he stared at her nose as he couldn't look her in the eyes, and her lips only reminded him that he would never be able to kiss them again.

"I'm sorry I ran off like that. It was just that the news shook me up so bad I couldn't think."

"It's understandable."

"I didn't mean to worry you." She took his hand in hers. "But I called the doctor's office and found out it's true. The test results were mixed up. I can have kids."

"I'm really happy for you." His flat tone probably told her how he really felt—miserable for himself.

"I'm really sorry for upsetting you."

"It's fine." He turned back toward the water, unable to even face her nose any longer.

She spoke, but he couldn't process what she said. Not when she'd chosen another. He held her no ill will, but it was becoming clearer by the second that he couldn't be around her.

He spun around and finally looked her in the eyes. "I can't do this. I've got to go."

Her mouth fell open. "What?"

"Goodbye, Maggie." He marched away, kicking up sand with each step.

"Canyon!" Maggie called. "I don't have your—"

He burst into a run before he had to face her again. Once in his car, he squealed the tires as he pulled out of the parking spot.

CHAPTER 31

M aggie stared at the parking spot that Canyon had just left.

That hadn't been the sweet reunion she'd pictured. She'd imagined him taking her into his arms and giving her that heartfelt kiss of his.

What happened? Where did she go wrong? Was it something she said? Or something she hadn't said? And how was she going to talk to him to work it out?

It was time to find out. She marched toward her car.

"Maggie!"

She spun around to see Isabella waving frantically.

"It's so good to see you!" Her friend ran over and nearly squeezed the air from Maggie's lungs as she hugged her.

That was more like the response she'd expected from Canyon.

"Everyone was so worried. You should've seen your auntie. She was madder than a wet hen."

Maggie frowned. "I really didn't mean to worry anyone. I just…" There was no time to get into it. Not when she needed to find Canyon. "Hey, I have to get going. If you see Canyon, can you tell him that I need to talk with him?"

"Sure. I have something to ask you when you get a minute."

"What?" Maggie asked.

"I want you to be one of my bridesmaids. It goes without saying but I wanted to officially ask if you would be one. It wouldn't feel right if you weren't standing with me."

"Oh, you're so sweet!" Maggie embraced her friend. "I would love to. I'm sorry to have to run, but I'm dealing with a little bit of an emergency."

Isabella's eyes widened. "Is everything okay?"

"I hope it will be. I'll call you soon."

"Anything I can do?"

"Just tell Canyon to call me if you see him." Maggie bolted toward her car before she could lose another moment.

"Can't you just—?"

Maggie would find out what she was asking later. She headed in the same direction Canyon went, but she'd lost so much time, it would be hard to find him if he didn't want to be found.

She wanted to drive faster but knew better than to speed through town. As she gripped the steering wheel, she kept looking for Canyon or his car. She saw neither.

Her mouth was like a parched desert, so she pulled into a spot in front of Sweet Caroline's. If nothing else, she could have Caroline tell Canyon she was looking for him.

"What can I get you, darlin'?" Caroline smiled at Maggie, but then it faded. "Is everything all right?"

Was she referring to Maggie's disappearance, or could she see Maggie was upset?

"I can't find Canyon."

Caroline shook her head. "You kids have to stop disappearing. First you, now him. Is he okay?"

"He didn't seem himself, then he just took off." Maggie took a deep breath. "It's complicated, but if you see him, can you tell him to call me? I lost his number. You don't happen to have it, do you, Miss Caroline?"

She shook her head. "I don't think I have his mama's number, either."

"It's okay, thanks." Maggie ordered a tea, then gulped it down as fast as she could before heading back to her car.

She drove to Canyon's house, but his car wasn't there. It wasn't at the little house or anywhere else in Indigo Bay as far as she could tell.

Her stomach twisted in knots, and she understood what everyone else had gone through the previous night when she'd been in that field.

If only she hadn't blocked Dan's number, she'd give him a piece of her mind for deleting all of Canyon's information from her phone. But it was for the best, because there was no way she was going to give him the satisfaction of knowing he'd actually managed to interfere with her getting ahold of Canyon.

After driving all over town twice, she stopped at the little house and went inside, despite not seeing Canyon's car.

Harry was painting the living room. He turned to her and smiled, a long streak of light green paint smeared across his face. "Hi, Maggie. Have you found Canyon?"

Disappointment washed through her. "I was going to ask you the same thing."

He shook his head. "Still hasn't come back since lunch."

"Do you have his number?"

Harry gave her a double-take. "You don't?"

"I did, but don't now. It's kind of complicated."

"Hold on." Harry set down the paintbrush, then wiped his hands on his overalls. "Let me grab my phone."

Maggie dug her phone out and waited eagerly for Harry to return to the living room.

He read out the number, then Maggie entered the number in again. She'd have to make a point to of memorizing it after she talked to Canyon. "Thank you so much, Harry!"

"Sure thing. Do me a favor and have him give me a call once you reach him."

"Definitely. Thanks again!" She raced outside, already calling Canyon.

Straight to voicemail. She threw back her head in frustration.

She sent him a text saying how much she wanted him to call her.

Now the question was what to do next. Should she keep looking for him, or should she go home and get some rest? She'd already scoured Indigo Bay. He either wasn't there, or he didn't want to be found.

Her phone rang.

Maggie whipped it up to check the caller ID. It was just Aunt Lucille.

"Hi, Auntie," she answered.

"Did you find Canyon?"

Technically she had, but didn't feel like getting into all the complicated details. "I'm trying to find him. If you see him, can you tell him to call me, please?"

"I will. I'm about to take Princess for a walk—she was just groomed, and I want to show off her new haircut. I'll be sure to keep an eye out for him."

"Thanks, Auntie. I appreciate it."

"Why don't you come home and rest? You've had quite the day."

Maggie yawned, despite her worry. "I might just do that. A nap sounds great." If her mind would let her sleep.

She said goodbye to her aunt, then trudged to her car. It felt like giving up, but Canyon obviously didn't want to be found.

Then she realized exactly where he had to be hiding.

CHAPTER 32

Canyon tossed the burger wrappers into the garbage and waved to the kid at the register. "Thanks."

The kid said something, but Canyon couldn't hear it over "Why do Fools Fall in Love?" blaring from the juke box. How fitting.

He went outside and stared at his car. The air itself seemed to crush him. Or was that his heart breaking? Either way, he was in no mood to get on the road.

There was a lot to figure out, and he needed air. Canyon tightened the laces on his shoes, then headed for the path leading to the waterfall.

Unfortunately, all along the way he could only think of his last hike—with Maggie. It had been wonderful, every-thing he'd ever dreamed that taking her there would be. But that one memory was all he would ever have now. She was probably planning her wedding with Dan as he made his way up the path.

Canyon shoved those thoughts aside, only to see a root sticking out. Maggie had stumbled over it, and he'd caught her. Then she'd given him her bright smile, and they'd laughed and shared a heart-exploding kiss.

He took a deep breath. Maybe going to the waterfall wasn't such a hot idea, after all. Instead of giving him something to think about, it would probably only remind him more of her.

In fact, everything in and around Indigo Bay would do that. The beach would only make him think of all their secret dates and the night they'd danced then talked by the water.

At least he'd had those two weeks with her. It was more than he'd ever thought he would get. They were from two different worlds, and he was lucky just to be one of her best friends for so many years. Dating her was something he didn't deserve.

Not that Dan did, either. But he was the one who could give her the life she was used to. They'd be able to send their future kids to an expensive private school and give them every opportunity under the sun.

What could Canyon give Maggie or any future children? Even if he worked long hours, he couldn't come close to providing what Dan could.

Stop!

Canyon tried once again to shove Maggie from his thoughts. It was pointless to think about her. They had no future together.

Why had he thought he actually had a chance with her? He'd have been so much better off never having reconnected with her. Knowing how good they'd been, what could've been, only made it hurt all the more.

He reached the waterfall and leaned against a tree.

What was he going to do now? If he stayed in Indigo Bay, everything would be like a slap in the face, reminding him of what he'd had but lost.

Even his job would be a constant reminder—the house

that had been for Maggie. Not that it would be any longer. No, she was probably already packing for Georgia if she wasn't already on the road.

His heart shattered all over again. It was becoming apparent that it could break time and time again.

Maybe what he needed was to go back to the cruise line. His boss *had* told Canyon that he could have his job back anytime he wanted it.

He didn't really want to go back, but it would be better than facing the soul-crushing reminders waiting for him back in Indigo Bay.

What other option did he have? At least he would be busy on the boat. He would hardly have a free moment to think about Maggie. It had been the perfect distraction all that time before, and it would work again.

He hoped. It had been one thing to hop on the ship and leave his memories of Maggie behind when he'd never experienced what it had been like to be loved by her. Now there was the chance that nothing could distract him. His thoughts would be on her as he worked himself to the bone, unable to push her aside.

Canyon would probably see her in other people—someone with similar eyes or a similar build. Nobody would have her smile. That was unique to her, especially the way her eyes lit up when she smiled at him.

But now she was going to look at Dan like that. Not Canyon.

No point in thinking about that. It was time to move on with his life, and for now that meant returning to the cruise ship. He just needed to get himself back to Florida.

He pulled out his phone and called his old boss. Voicemail. Not that that was surprising. There was no cell coverage out at sea.

Canyon left a quick message, then called Archer, but his

number went to voicemail. He must be back at work. It had been a couple weeks since he'd called.

Were any of his other friends taking a week off? Or maybe he could just find a club or party to hang out at to forget his problems. Anything would be better than this.

Not that partying could completely make him forget how much he loved Maggie, but it would be enough of a distraction that it wouldn't hurt as much for a while. Eventually it would stop hurting altogether.

Right?

Canyon stared at the waterfall as if it could give him the answers he needed. It didn't. He kicked some rocks, then headed down a different path than the one he'd taken. The last thing he needed was another trip down memory lane.

It was a steeper, rockier path, but at least the only thing it would remind him of would be tromping around with his brother. The brother that he hadn't talked to in years.

Canyon really needed to give him a call. He also really needed to get out of South Carolina and back to Florida. The open sea would be like returning to a friend with arms wide open, welcoming him back. All he needed to do was to get back home, throw his few belongings into his car, and take off.

But no, he didn't want to go back to his old life. He'd already learned that it wouldn't replace Maggie. There had to be another option.

And there was, but it made his stomach twist in knots.

Canyon could call his brother. They were out of state, running a father-and-son plumbing business. He would have to swallow a lot of pride to call them but at least he wouldn't have to face Indigo Bay.

He pulled out his phone and found Dayton's number. His pulse drummed in his ear as his thumb hovered over the call button. He closed his eyes and tapped it.

The phone immediately started ringing. Canyon hadn't been blocked!

"Canyon?"

Dayton's familiar voice soothed all of Canyon's worries. "Yeah, Dayton. It's me. How are you?"

"Great. A little surprised, I have to admit."

Guilt stung Canyon. He was as guilty for their estrangement as his brother. In fact, he couldn't even remember what had started the whole thing. Canyon raked his fingers through his hair and cleared his throat. "I was thinking of heading your way. You got a couch I can crash on, by chance?"

"I'd give you my bed! Get your butt over here."

"Wait. Seriously?"

Dayton laughed. "Are you kidding me? I haven't seen my brother in years."

Canyon's mind raced. This was perfect. Not only would he be able to stay with Dayton—at least for a little while—but he was eager to see him!

"When will you be here?" Dayton asked.

"Um, let me call in an hour or two."

"Sounds great. I can't wait to see you! Dad's missed you, too."

"He has?"

"Well, he hasn't said anything. You know him. But I can tell. He keeps your picture on his desk."

"Wow. I don't know what to say."

"Say you'll bring pizza."

Canyon laughed. "Okay. I'll bring pizza."

"Perfect. Talk in an hour or so."

They said their goodbyes, then Canyon leaned against a tree and let the news sink in. His dad and brother actually wanted to see him.

He'd just filled the fridge and paid rent to his mom, so she would be fine. Probably wouldn't even miss him.

Now it was just a matter of getting out of Indigo Bay without another unwanted trip down memory lane.

CHAPTER 33

Maggie pulled into the parking lot at the little fifties diner. Relief swept through her when she saw Canyon's car parked in the back corner.

She bolted out of her car and glanced over at his. Not seeing him in it, she raced inside. "Splish Splash" blared from the juke box. She looked around, not seeing him, then rushed to the counter.

A bored-looking teen glanced over at her. "What can I get you?"

"Have you seen Canyon?"

"The Grand Canyon?"

Maggie groaned and found a picture of him on her phone. "No. This guy. Was he in here?"

The kid glanced at the picture. "Yeah. He left a little while ago."

He'd already left? But his car was in the parking lot. She hadn't missed him, had she?

The waterfall! He had to have gone there.

"Thanks!" She spun around and raced out of the restaurant.

Canyon's car was still there. Her sandals weren't the best for hiking, but she'd be fine. She broke into a sprint toward the path she'd taken with him before.

Everything had been going so well the last time. If only she knew what had gone wrong in the last day—other than Dan showing up. Obviously, seeing him threw them both off despite the news that he could've just told her over the phone. Did he really think Maggie would go back to him?

She shuddered at the thought. Him figuring out her passcode, or somehow finding a way around it, showed Maggie just how much better off she was without him. Actually, no. Everything about Canyon showed her how much better off she was without Dan.

Maggie's feet blistered, and she broke out into a sweat as she made her way through the trail. She made sure to avoid some exposed roots as she continued on.

At last, the sounds of the waterfall. Maggie gasped for air and picked up her pace.

She was almost there. The muscles in her legs burned, protesting. She pressed on, working them harder. Later, after working things out with Canyon, she could give them a break.

The path twisted and turned some more before the work of nature finally appeared.

Maggie raced for it and looked around. Canyon wasn't there.

"Canyon!"

The waterfall muffled her cry. She raced around to the other side and searched behind every tree.

He was nowhere.

How had she missed him? She'd taken the exact trail they'd taken the other day.

Unless there was another one that she didn't know about. He'd come here often as a kid with his brother. He probably knew the whole area really well—and if he was trying to avoid her, what better way than to take a path she didn't know about?

"Canyon!"

If he was nearby, he wasn't coming out. All she managed to do was to scare some birds who flew away when she called out his name.

Her heart thundered in her chest and desperation ran through her. A path tucked away almost behind the waterfall caught her attention.

Could that be where he'd gone? It seemed to go in the opposite direction as the restaurant. Maybe that was it, especially if he wanted to get away from everything and think.

If that was the case, should she leave him alone? She hadn't wanted anyone around the night before, so she could understand the need for space.

As much as Maggie wanted to dart down the path, she hesitated. She didn't want to invade his space if he needed time alone. He probably needed to process everything that had happened in the last day. It was a lot to take in.

She pulled out her phone and texted a quick message saying she wanted to talk to him. After pressing send, the message got stuck halfway through sending.

It was a really weak signal. She'd have to get back to the parking lot before it would send.

Maggie glanced back and forth between the path near the waterfall and the one she'd taken. One *might* lead her to Canyon but the other one would definitely take her to cell reception.

Something rustled behind her.

She spun around, heart pounding. Could it be Canyon, or was it someone else? She was out in the woods without anything to protect herself.

More rustling.

Her throat closed up. She wanted to scream, but her voice wouldn't cooperate. Her feet wouldn't move. In fact, the blisters throbbed and her leg muscles ached.

What if it was a wild animal? Or a predator in the human form?

More rustling noises.

She spun around and ran toward the trail she'd taken to get there.

"Maggie?"

She froze.

"What are you doing here?"

Maggie turned back around slowly.

Canyon stood by the waterfall. Twigs and leaves were stuck in his hair and mud covered his clothes.

"What happened to you?"

"Let's just say the path hasn't been well maintained while I've been gone."

"Are you okay?"

"I'm fine. What are you doing out here?" He frowned.

"Looking for you."

"Why?" His tone was rough.

"Because we need to talk."

Canyon's expression contorted. "About what?"

He may as well have slapped her across the face. "What do you mean? About us?"

"Don't you mean Dan?"

"What? No."

"You don't want to talk about him?" Canyon's brows knitted together.

"What's going on, Canyon?"

"I don't know. Why don't you tell me?"

She took a deep breath. "That's all I've been doing. You were acting strange at the beach before running off, then I ran all over Indigo Bay trying to find you before realizing you had to be here."

He shrugged.

With each indifferent word and gesture, her heart broke more and more. She blinked back tears. "Why are you acting like this?"

"Like what?" He crossed his arms and leaned against a tree.

"This! Angry and refusing to tell me what's going on."

"Me? You're going to put this on me?"

"You're acting weird, and I can't for the life of me figure out why!" A lump formed in her throat. She wouldn't be able to hold back the tears much longer.

"*I'm* the one acting weird? Unbelievable!"

"Just tell me what's going on!"

"What's to tell? You're going back to Dan!"

She stared at him, trying to digest his words. "What? Why do you think that?"

"Oh, I don't know. Maybe the text you sent me. Or Dan answering Lucille's door and telling me you chose him. Any of this ringing a bell?"

Everything spun around as Canyon's words filled in all the blanks. Dan had texted Canyon while he'd had her phone and he'd answered the door and spewed more lies.

It all made sense. Except why Canyon believed any of it could be true.

"You don't have anything to say?" His mouth formed a straight line as he glared at her.

Maggie stepped closer and studied his jaded expression, and it became clear why he'd believed it.

Underneath the tough exterior, he was hurt. It shone through his eyes. Canyon could hide it everywhere else, but the window to his soul gave him away.

She took a few more steps toward him. "I never sent that text."

Canyon flinched but didn't say anything.

"I also didn't know Dan answered the door, or that you were there."

"Why was he staying there?"

"Aunt Lucille invited him. I locked myself in my room to stay as far from him as I could."

Different expressions flickered across Canyon's face. "So, what's really going on?"

Maggie closed the distance between them, not leaving much space at all. "He showed up, thinking I'd run back to him—something that would never happen."

"Why'd you run off last night?"

"I needed to get away and think. To process what he'd said about the test results being wrong."

They held each other's gazes. Canyon's expression softened with each passing moment.

"You're saying that at no point did you consider going back to him?"

Maggie scrunched her face. "Never. If he was the last man on earth and I was the last woman, humanity would be doomed."

The corners of Canyon's mouth twitched. "Really?"

"I swear." Maggie put her hand on his arm. "I only want to be with you."

He stared at her with a deep intensity in his eyes, then pulled her into his embrace. His heart thundered in her ear.

CHAPTER 34

C anyon held Maggie tightly and breathed in her sweet scent. It was a fruity combination of her hair and perfume. His heart warmed, and his entire body relaxed having her so close.

Everything felt right in the world again. Especially knowing everything Dan had said was nothing but lies.

Canyon should've known. He should've fought harder for the woman he loved.

He ran his hands over the length of her hair. "Can you forgive me for being an idiot?"

"You're not an idiot."

"I believed Dan instead of insisting on finding out the truth from you."

She looked up at him. "You thought that text was from me. What did it say?"

He frowned. "Basically, that you'd chosen him."

Maggie's beautiful face contorted in anger. "What did I ever see in him? I don't even know how he got my phone. It was locked in my room and it had my passcode on it."

"People like him find ways of getting what they want no

matter what it takes. You might want to make sure there isn't any spyware on it. I'd hate to think he installed something like that."

Her eyes widened. "You think he would?"

"You think he wouldn't?"

Maggie frowned. "I'm really sorry for everything, Canyon."

He cupped her chin. "It's not your fault. Let's just hope he decides to stay away."

"After what Aunt Lucille said to him, I'm sure he will."

Canyon chuckled. "I can imagine. That woman can be scary."

"Just don't tell her that." Maggie laughed.

His heart warmed at the sound. "Oh, I'm sure she knows."

"That's true." She leaned her head against his shoulder.

Canyon held her, never wanting to let go. "Where did you go last night? Nobody could find you anywhere."

"It's going to sound stupid."

"Why?"

"I found an empty field outside of town, and I sat there just thinking until I fell asleep. The last thing I wanted was to worry anyone. I just needed to process everything without anyone around."

Canyon kissed her temple. "I understand, but next time can you tell someone where you're going?"

Maggie nodded. "Hopefully that's the last time I receive news so mind-blowing."

He cupped her chin again and stared into her eyes. "Did you confirm that he was telling the truth? About the medical report, I mean."

"Yeah. I spoke with the doctor's office. It's some other poor woman who can't have kids. I'm perfectly fine."

"You certainly are."

Pink colored her cheeks.

Canyon laughed. "You're so easy to embarrass."

She shrugged.

"I hope you know that any man would be lucky to marry you, whether you could have kids or not."

Maggie looked away.

He kissed her cheek. "It's the truth. I'd marry you in a heartbeat, and the news of your test hasn't changed that one bit."

She turned back to look at him, her eyes huge. "You want to marry me?"

"I'd be the luckiest man alive."

Tears shone in her eyes.

Canyon brushed his lips across hers. She kissed him back eagerly, and her tears spilled onto his cheeks. He opened his eyes and kissed her tears from her eyes.

She smiled at him, a tear clinging to the lash.

A crazy idea flashed through his mind. He had to follow it.

Canyon cleared his throat, then stepped back. His pulse raced through him as he lowered himself to one knee.

Maggie's mouth dropped open. "What are you doing?"

He took her hand in his. "I may not be rich or hand-some, and I won't be able to buy you nice things, but there is one thing I can give you. My heart. It's already yours, Mags. It has been since we were kids running around the beach. You're the only one I've ever loved even though I always thought you were out of my reach. If you marry me, I promise to love you every day and treat you like a princess."

"Canyon—"

"I'm not done. The last two weeks with you has been a dream come true. Something I never thought I'd get to expe-rience. I know this is sudden, and we haven't been dating all that long, so we can have a long engagement. But please say you'll marry me. I'll never take you for granted, and I'll appreciate you always."

"I—"

"And I'll get you a ring. A beautiful one. I just need some time to save up for the down payment. And—"

"Yes! I'll marry you, Canyon. Happily!"

He rose to his feet and kissed her. The whole world melted away other than the sounds of the rushing waterfall off to the side.

She'd actually agreed to his spur-of-the-moment proposal!

Magnolia Lucille Kendrick had agreed to marry him.

One moment he'd thought he'd lost her forever and the next she had agreed to spend the rest of her life with him.

He pulled back and stared at the gorgeous smiling face of his fiancée. It hardly seemed real, but it was true.

Canyon brushed some dirt from his shirt. He'd slipped off a narrow path, down into a muddy ravine. "Sorry to be such a mess for the proposal."

She pulled a twig from his hair. "It's perfect."

"Perfect?" He laughed, then felt his hair, which had more twigs stuck in it. "I'm a wreck."

"A perfect wreck. I think that fits us, don't you?"

He traced her jawline with his thumb. "You're not."

"I am."

"No, you're perfect and I'm a wreck. A perfect wreck describes us to a tee."

She pulled more things from his hair and kissed his nose. "I suppose we'll have to agree to disagree."

"Maybe."

CHAPTER 35

T*wo months later.*

Canyon wiped his brow after walking through the little house.

"Not bad, huh?" Harry grinned.

"It looks like a whole new home."

"That it does. It's going to be the perfect starter home for some newlyweds."

Canyon beamed. Even after being engaged for two months, he still hadn't wrapped his mind around the fact that he and Maggie would soon be living there as husband and wife.

"You still planning to help with the yellow cottage over on Seaside Boulevard?"

"I'll be there bright and early Monday morning."

Harry put a hand on Canyon's shoulder. "You're a great worker. I wish you'd consider coming on as a permanent hire."

"I'll keep that in mind as a backup plan."

"How's the dance studio coming?"

"Maggie and I have it up to tip-top shape. Mostly her, though. While I'm here, she's working hard over there."

Harry nodded. "I'm sure the kids around town will have a blast taking lessons from you two."

"What I can't believe is that we already have a waitlist. Everyone in Indigo Bay seems to want dance lessons."

"A waitlist? Maybe you'd better add me to it. My wife has been nudging me to sign up at your studio."

Canyon grinned. "Really? We've been talking about a couples' class if there's enough interest. I'll put you two down for sure."

"Thanks. I'll be sure to tell her. Have a great weekend."

"You too, Harry."

"Oh, these are yours." Harry pulled a key off his keychain. "Congrats on your new home."

Canyon's heart swelled. He'd been half-expecting to wake up and find it all to be a dream. But it wasn't. Maggie still hadn't backed out from his proposal by the waterfall.

He said goodbye to Harry, locked the front door—his future front door—and headed to his car.

A text came in from Maggie.

Maggie: Still on for tonight?

Canyon: I'll be there at exactly six.

Maggie: Can't wait! Xoxo

Canyon: Me too.

He added in some kissing emojis before climbing into his car and heading home to get cleaned up. In an hour, he and Maggie were having dinner at Lucille's again.

At precisely six o'clock, he rang the doorbell.

The door flung open before he'd even let go of the bell, and Maggie threw her arms around him. "I missed you so much!"

He kissed her and winked. "It's been torture since lunch."

"Come on in. Auntie ordered Chinese—with chopsticks. I'm sure you'll both get a good laugh out of my attempts."

Canyon threaded his fingers through hers. "I would never laugh at you."

"You might just eat those words. I've been practicing, but it hasn't helped."

"I'm sure you're better than you give yourself credit for." Canyon held out a chair at the table for Maggie. Once she was seated, he helped Lucille pour the takeout into fancy dishes. Out of the corner of his eye, he watched Maggie practicing with the chopsticks.

As soon as she had food piled on her plate, she picked up a piece of sour chicken and ate it just as well as Canyon, who had been using chopsticks for years.

"I'm impressed."

"Oh, stop."

"No, really. I am." He glanced over at Lucille, who appeared amused watching them.

After everyone was done, Maggie stretched. "I ate too much. I could go for a walk on the beach." She turned to her aunt. "Can I help with the dishes?"

"Not tonight. I've got it. You two enjoy the night."

"Thanks, Auntie." Maggie slid her hand into Canyon's, and they strolled out of the kitchen. Before they reached the front door, Lucille stepped in front of them.

She stared down Canyon. "Come with me. We need to talk about something before you two leave."

His heart skipped a beat and he glanced at Maggie. "Um, okay."

"You don't have to ask her for permission. Follow me." She nodded at Maggie. "We'll only be a moment."

"Sure, Auntie."

Canyon squeezed Maggie's hand, then followed Lucille up the stairs and into an elegant bedroom. "Miss Lucille?"

"We're practically family. You can drop the *Miss*."

"Okay."

She strolled over to a desk and opened a drawer.

Canyon studied her, his mind racing as he tried to figure out what was going on.

Lucille rifled through the contents before pulling something out. A tall jewelry box hid whatever she was now looking at.

"Come over here."

He held his breath as he made his way over.

"Sit." She nodded toward the bed.

Canyon sat, still unable to see what was in Lucille's hands.

She met his gaze and waited a beat before speaking. "I have to admit to being nervous about you and my Maggie being together."

He nodded. "You made your feelings toward me clear."

Lucille smiled. "But Maggie convinced me to give you a chance. I worried every time she left with you, but you've proven yourself to be a man of good character. You treat the both of us with the utmost respect."

Canyon swallowed and waited for her to continue.

"You've won me over. I couldn't be happier to have you marry my sweet niece."

"Thank you, ma'am."

"If I don't want you calling me miss, I definitely don't want you calling me ma'am."

"Sorry. What would you like me to call you?"

"Aunt Lucille is fine."

"Okay, Mi—Aunt Lucille."

She walked over, her hands clasped together. "I want to give this to you. For you to give to Maggie. Hold out your hand."

Canyon opened his palm, and she dropped a ring onto it. It was silver with an enormous diamond in the middle and a swirly pattern around it filled with smaller rocks. The sides had intricate carvings that matched the front design. It was elegant enough for a princess.

"It was my engagement ring, and I've been widowed for two decades. I'd say it's time the ring gets some use, wouldn't you?"

He glanced up at her, unable to find his voice. "You... you're giving this to me?"

"I know you've been saving for a ring. Use the money for the honeymoon or put it toward that dance academy."

"I... I don't know what to say. You've already gifted us the house."

"I'd give the world for Maggie. She's like a daughter to me, and you're quickly growing on me, as well. If you like it, I want you both to have it. I'll give you the matching wedding band on the wedding day."

Canyon picked up the ring and held it between his first finger and his thumb. "What's not to like? It's beautiful, and more importantly, I know Maggie will love it."

"She was often entranced by it as a small child when she would visit us." A sadness crossed Lucille's face and she looked lost in thought. "Well, enough of that. Let's go downstairs. When do you think you'll give it to her?"

"Right away. She's engaged and should have a ring to show off."

"At least take her somewhere special. Go to the water or somewhere else you two enjoy."

"Thank you, Aunt Lucille." He wrapped his arms around her.

"My pleasure." She returned the embrace, then they headed back downstairs.

Canyon tucked the ring safely in a pocket before reaching the first level.

"I have somewhere to be now," Lucille announced. "You two have a good rest of the night."

"Thanks, Auntie." Maggie kissed her on the cheek.

Canyon gave her a little nod, his pulse racing at the thought of giving the ring to Maggie. Should he propose again or simply surprise her with it?

Lucille headed back upstairs, her little white dog following at her heels.

He turned to Maggie. "Would you like to go to the beach? Maybe to our secret spot?"

She held his hand. "I'd like that."

Canyon nodded, then they walked toward the back door for easier access to the beach. His pulse drummed faster. He was more nervous about this than he had been proposing—that'd been spur of the moment.

Halfway to the beach, she turned to him. "Are you okay? You're awfully quiet."

He smiled. "Just enjoying your company."

Maggie squeezed his hand but didn't look like she believed him.

Once they reached their spot, she leaned against him and wrapped her arms around him. "This is nice, and you know what's even better?"

"What's that?"

She looked up at him, beaming. "We don't have to hide our love from anyone."

"About that…" He stepped back and dug into his pocket.

Maggie tilted her head and scrunched her brow.

His pulse was out of control. It was so loud, he couldn't hear any other noise at the beach. He fumbled with the ring in his pocket, then took a deep breath before pulling it out.

Her eyes widened and she covered her mouth.

Canyon knelt on one knee. "I love you more than life itself, Maggie, and I'm the luckiest man alive because I get to marry you. You deserve nothing other than the best, and now you can at least have a ring that comes close to matching your beauty."

Tears shone in her eyes.

He took her hand and slid on the ring. By some miracle, it was a perfect fit.

Maggie held it up, studying it. "It's so gorgeous, I just can't believe…" Her voice trailed off and her eyes widened. "Is that Aunt Lucille's?"

Canyon rose and kissed her. "It was, but now it's yours. She wants us to have it."

"I never thought she'd part with it. She's never even entertained the idea of remarrying that I'm aware of, so I never thought she'd let go of this ring."

"She seemed really happy to pass it along to you."

Maggie threw her arms around him and held him tightly. "She must really believe in us. You've done well at winning her over."

"More importantly, I've won *you* over."

She grinned and gave him another kiss.

He was definitely the luckiest guy in the world.

EPILOGUE

Maggie smiled as they pulled up to their little home. Canyon turned to her, squeezed her hand, and kissed it. Then he climbed out and opened the door for her.

She stretched her legs and took in the sight. It was nice to be home.

Canyon opened the back passenger door. Little Lucy scrambled out and called for the cat. Canyon went over to the other side and pulled out the baby car seat.

Maggie went over and kissed him, then their newborn boy. She reached for the car seat handle, but Canyon shook his head.

"You aren't supposed to carry it yet."

She was about to protest when Lucy called out, "Mama! Daddy! Come look at this!"

Maggie closed the car door.

They found their daughter jumping up and down near a bush. "Look! Emma had her kitties! Just like you, Mama."

Maggie ruffled the three-year-old's hair. "Luckily, I just had one."

"We have kitties *and* a baby!"

Canyon laughed. "I think you're more excited about the kittens than your baby brother."

"Oh, Daddy. You're just silly." She threw him an exasperated glance. "Are we going to bring them inside?"

"We probably should, but first, the baby."

After Lucy had given her new brother a tour of the house, she and Canyon brought the kittens and their mama inside. Lucy bounced around, so excited she could hardly contain herself.

Maggie watched Lucy, her heart filled to overflowing. It was hard to believe there had been a time she'd thought a family would be out of her future. Now she had not one, but two wonderful children and a husband who adored both of them and her.

Little Nolan finally woke, and Maggie pulled her son from the car seat. Lucy ran over, her long hair flying behind her, and chatted a mile-a-minute to her brother, telling him all about the kittens.

Nolan stared at her as though taking in every word, then let out a cry.

Lucy's eyes widened. "Did I break him?"

Maggie kissed her cheek. "I think he's hungry. I'll feed him, then you can finish your story."

"Okay." Lucy skipped away.

Maggie made herself comfortable, then nursed the baby.

Canyon plopped next to her. "If I didn't know better, I'd think Aunt Lucille gave Lucy several cups of coffee before we picked her up."

Maggie grinned. "She's just excited. Kittens and a new baby all in one day."

He yawned. "At least she should sleep well tonight. She'll probably be the only one."

Ding-dong!

Maggie and Canyon exchanged a glance.

"Are we expecting anyone?" she asked.

"Not that I'm aware." He patted her knee. "I'll get it."

"Oh, hi!" Canyon said. "What's this?"

Maggie craned her neck but couldn't see the door from where she sat.

"Dolly Mayes is here." Canyon poked his head around the corner. "Is it okay if she comes in?"

"Of course." Maggie covered the nursing baby. "Come on, Dolly!"

The tall redhead came over, carrying a large brown box. "This is from all the families at the dance studio, darlin'. Enough food to feed your family for a week!"

"You're so sweet." Maggie beamed. "Thank you."

"Everyone wanted to come and see you and Nolan, but that can wait until you settle in. Mind if I get these meals in the fridge?"

"Go right ahead."

Dolly rushed into the kitchen. "Shall I warm one of these up now?"

"That'd be great," Maggie called. "I'm famished. Hospital food leaves a lot to be desired."

Dolly laughed. "Isn't that the truth?"

Canyon came over and gave Maggie a quick kiss. "Wasn't that nice of them?"

"It sure was. I'm too tired to even think about cooking."

He put his arm around her. "And you know I won't let you cook while you're busy taking care of a newborn."

Dolly appeared. "All set! The timer should go off in about forty minutes. It's my special pot roast and grits recipe. Enjoy!"

"Thank you, Dolly."

"Don't mention it. Congrats, you two!" She blew Maggie a kiss before heading out the door.

Canyon drew in a deep breath. "I'm exhausted. I can't imagine how you feel."

"I'm on cloud nine." She gave him a quick kiss.

Knock, knock!

They exchanged a glance.

"Who now?" Canyon asked.

Maggie handed the baby to him. "I'll get it this time."

"You don't have to."

"I know I don't have to. I want to." She plodded over to the front door and opened it.

Her brother-in-law and father-in-law stood on the door, both holding presents wrapped in baby-blue paper.

She grinned. "Canyon didn't tell me you two were coming to town!"

"He didn't know. I heard my grandson is home and I dropped everything." Felton Leblanc wrapped his arms around Maggie. "Is the boy ready to meet his grandpa and uncle?"

Maggie squeezed him back, then gave Dayton a warm hug and waved them in.

They both greeted Canyon warmly, then fawned over Nolan. Lucy heard the commotion and ran into the room and nearly knocked over Dayton with a hug.

Their home was filled with laughter and family. Maggie's heart was fuller than she ever imagined it could be.

Canyon put his arm around Maggie. "This is the life, isn't it? A gorgeous wife, two beautiful kids, extended family, and even clients who love us like family. What more could we ask for?"

She kissed him, scratching her cheek on the scruff on his face. "Nothing. Nothing at all."

THE HUNTERS

If you enjoyed *Sweet Reunion*, you're sure to love reading about the tight-knit Hunter family as they find their loves in their seaside town!

You can start at the beginning, or you can start where we first get to know Cassidy and her doggie paradise in *Bayside Destinies*. But she hasn't found her happily ever after yet… It will be coming soon in *Bayside Dreams*.

The Seaside Hunters

Seaside Surprises

Work hard. Play often. Love unconditionally.

Tiffany Saunders is on the run. When she winds up stranded in a seaside town, she wants nothing more than to forget her horrific past and kept moving. But a chance meeting with a handsome local changes everything.

Jake Hunter has some deep emotional scars and is trying to cope with running the family business. The last thing he wants is a relationship—until a mysterious brunette walks into his store and complicates it all.

Tiffany prefers to keep the painful memories of the past where they belong—in her rear view mirror. But dark secrets cannot stay hidden forever. Just as the walls around Tiffany's heart start to come down, the past catches up with her. Will true love be able to conquer all?

Seaside Heartbeats

Sometimes love shows up when you least expect it.

After years of hard work, architect Lana Summers just wants a relaxing vacation in the beach town of Kittle Falls. Instead, she suffers unexpected heart problems, and finds herself in the office of a gorgeous cardiologist—who only makes her heart work harder.

Brayden Hunter left his successful cardiology practice in Dallas to be closer to his aging parents. Focused on building a health care clinic in his hometown, he doesn't want any distractions. However, the beautiful Lana is one he can't seem to avoid.

As their attraction grows, they stumble upon a 160-year-old mystery. Brayden catches her adventurous spirit as they chase after answers, and he can't help falling for her. But can he convince her to stay in the small beach town and with him?

Seaside Dances

Dream big. Dance often. Love completely.

Zachary Hunter is no stranger to rejection. After multiple failed efforts to get his novel published in New York, he's counting on a trip home to turn his luck around.

Jasmine Blackwell has big dreams. She hopes her internship as a dance instructor in Kittle Falls will be the stepping stone she needs to achieve her lifelong goals.

After a chance meeting, neither Zachary nor Jasmine can deny their attraction. They fear their aspirations are too big to let a relationship tie them down. Can they have both love and the careers of their dreams?

Seaside Kisses

People change, but some feelings last forever.

Rafael Hunter never thought he'd return to Kittle Falls, but life gave him no other choice. Los Angeles chewed him up, spit him out, and sent him back to square one.

Amara Fowler has lived in the small beach town her entire life. She's overcome her shyness to grow into the woman she always knew she could be, but she never forgot her secret crush. When the alluring Rafael returns, he can't help but stir in her a whirlwind of old feelings.

They've both changed so much. Has life kept them incompatible or has it molded them into a matching set?

Seaside Christmas

He can't stand her. She thinks he's crazy. Will their feelings stay etched in permanent ink?

Cruz Hunter has always stuck out in his small hometown. Now that he's covered in tattoos, the residents peg him as even more of an outcast. It seems like the whole world is against his dream of opening a local tattoo parlor.

When he finally finds the perfect place for his new business, Cruz discovers a pastor and his daughter have already bought it. The only thing more irritating than the change in his plan is Talia, a beautiful and feisty argument in a dress. Cruz would like nothing more than to have her out of his life and his mind, but for some reason, she's the only thing he can think about.

If Cruz and Talia can stop arguing long enough, opposites may do much more than attract.

Short Stories

Seaside Beginnings

This is the story of Robert and Dawn, the five Hunter brothers' parents. We meet them in each of the Seaside books, and they've grown on readers almost as much as the brothers themselves. Now we get a glimpse into their story.

Seaside Memories

Sophia is the youngest of the Hunter siblings. Each of her brothers hold her memory in a special place. Her story is one of first love, second chances, and enjoying life.

Seaside Treasures

Allen and Jackie's story is of an unlikely love and healing old wounds. They couldn't be more different, but that could be exactly what they need.

Read these and many other short stories in Tiny Bites, a snack-sized multi-genre collection by Stacy Claflin.

The Bayside Hunters

If you enjoyed falling for the Seaside Hunters, you'll love their Oregon cousins just as much. We've already met Logan, Sullivan, and Dakota. They and their two other siblings—twins, Freya and Shale—are about to find the loves of *their* lives… they just don't know it yet.

Bayside Wishes

She's guarding a family secret. He's investigating a murder. Will a second homecoming lead to true love?

Freya Hunter is living the fabulous life. The west-coast girl rakes it in as a fashion model in New York City, but everything changes after she returns home for a quick visit.

The reunion with friends and family in Enchantment Bay is sweet, especially when she hits it off with Nico Valentin, a ruggedly handsome police sergeant. As Nico investigates a murder, Freya learns a family secret big enough to turn her world upside down.

Freya is torn between her new life and her hometown — the life she loves vs. the brother who needs her and the sergeant who wants her. When her decision doesn't go nearly as well as she planned, she wonders if she can help her brother and keep her growing feelings for Nico at bay before they consume her.

Bayside Evenings

She's single and stuck. His relationship is going nowhere. Will the next wedding they plan... be their own?

Dakota Hunter is great at wedding planning but terrible at finding a guy. Each one she encounters is worse than the one before... until she meets Clay. There's one teensy problem: her attractive new assistant has a long-term girlfriend.

Clay Harper is thrilled to land his new job with Dakota, surrounding himself with happy couples day in and day out. But when he sees true love in person, he realizes his own relationship is far less than happy. It doesn't help that being around Dakota feels easy. It feels right.

As Dakota and Clay grow a deeper connection, Clay's girlfriend refuses to go down without a fight. Can the wedding planners go from seeing happy couples... to being one?

Bayside Promises

She's wounded. He's driven. Could they be exactly what the other needs?

Ten years earlier, Haley Faraway fled home without looking back. After her father's death, she reluctantly returns to Enchantment Bay to help her mom and sister. Painful memories haunt her, and Haley finds herself pouring her heart out to the one person she least expected—the impossibly gorgeous, albeit short-tempered, Sullivan Hunter.

Sullivan wants nothing more than to focus on his newly-acquired realty business. But when Haley comes back to town, he can't deny his attraction to her. After a string of bad relationships with gold-digging women, she's a breath of fresh air. Or is she? Just as he begins to get comfortable with their burgeoning relationship, he discovers she's a realtor, too. His temper gets the best of him as he suspects he's being used by yet another woman.

Every time Haley and Sullivan clear one hurdle, another looms larger in their path and they push each other away. Can they move on from from their painful pasts and find love—or are they doomed to repeat old mistakes?

Bayside Destinies

What do a fifteen-year-old pact, a fake engagement, and a stalker have in common? Audrey Hughes.

Audrey's ex-boyfriend won't take 'no' for an answer. A master manipulator and a violently selfish man, he's decided Audrey is his property. And he's determined to get her back. Forcibly, if necessary.

She flees to the one place she ever found 'family'—to Enchantment Bay. More precisely, to Logan Hunter.

Logan is a successful attorney and consummate bachelor. His work is his wife, and that's the only long-term relationship he sees for himself. Until a childhood sweetheart shows up and reminds him of the pact they made years earlier—to get married.

It surprises him that she remembered, stuns him that he's intrigued, and shocks him to discover her reason for returning. He uses all his influence and connections to protect her, only to be the one who causes her unbearable pain and drives her away.

Can Logan find a way to keep Audrey safe, make things right, and mend both their broken hearts?

Secret Jaguar

Valhalla's Curse

Renegade Valkyrie

Pursued Valkyrie

The Transformed Series

Main Series

Deception

Betrayal

Forgotten

Ascension

Duplicity

Sacrifice

Destroyed

Transcend

Entangled

Dauntless

Obscured

Partition

Standalones

Fallen

Silent Bite

Hidden Intentions

Saved by a Vampire

Sweet Desire

Short Story Collection

Tiny Bites

Standalones

Haunted

Love's First Kiss

Fall into Romance

AUTHOR'S NOTE

Thanks so much for reading *Sweet Reunion*. I hope you enjoyed reading Maggie and Canyon's story as much as I enjoyed writing it!

It was fun to write about Miss Lucille trying to push Maggie on Jace in *Sweet Dreams* last year. It was even more fun when I brought up the idea of other authors in the Indigo Bay series using the same storyline - and they loved the idea! Once it grew into a "thing" in the series, I knew I had to give poor Maggie her own happily ever after... and now she has it!

If you enjoyed this book, please consider leaving a review wherever you purchased it. Your review will help other readers find my work. Reviews can be short—just share your honest thoughts. That's it.

Want to know when I have a new release? Visit www.stacy-claflin.com for new release updates. You'll even get three free books!

Thank you for your support!

~Stacy

Made in the USA
Monee, IL
16 February 2021